KT-389-762

Welcome to...

The Hollywood Hills Clinic

*Where doctors to the stars
work miracles by day—
and explore their hearts' desires by night...*

When hotshot doc James Rothsberg
started the clinic six years ago
he dreamed of a world-class facility,
catering to Hollywood's biggest celebrities,
and his team are unrivalled in their fields.
Now, as the glare of the media spotlight
grows, the Hollywood Hills Clinic is
teaming up with the pro-bono
Bright Hope Clinic, and James is reunited
with Dr Mila Brightman...
the woman he jilted at the altar!

When it comes to juggling the care of
Hollywood A-listers with care for the
underprivileged kids of LA *anything* can
happen...and sizzling passions run high
in the shadow of the red carpet. With
everything at stake for James, Mila and the
Hollywood Hills Clinic medical team their
biggest challenges have only just begun!

Find out what happens in the dazzling

The Hollywood Hills Clinic miniseries

Available in Large Print format
from October 2016!

Dear Reader,

I was thrilled to be asked to write the first story in The Hollywood Hills Clinic series. It was wonderful to work with so many amazing authors and to hear the exciting plans that they had for their characters.

I always start out with a clear plan for my heroes and heroines, and then they just tend to stray off-course—but never more so than Freya and Zack. I kept trying to warn them that they might live to regret their one night of sizzling passion. They chose not to listen!

Truly, I don't blame them a bit.

I can't wait to read the entire continuity and see how the other heroes and heroines behaved.

Or not!

Happy reading!

Carol x

SEDUCED BY THE HEART SURGEON

BY
CAROL MARINELLI

MILLS
BOON

First published in Great Britain 2016
By Mills & Boon, an imprint of HarperCollins*Publishers*
1 London Bridge Street, London, SE1 9GF

Large Print edition 2016

© 2016 Harlequin Books S.A.

*Special thanks and acknowledgement are given
to Carol Marinelli for her contribution to*
The Hollywood Hills Clinic *series.*

ISBN: 978-0-263-26122-6

Our policy is to use papers that are natural, renewable and recyclable products and made from wood grown in sustainable forests. The logging and manufacturing processes conform to the legal environmental regulations of the country of origin.

Printed and bound in Great Britain
by CPI Antony Rowe, Chippenham, Wiltshire

Carol Marinelli recently filled in a form asking for her job title. Thrilled to be able to put down her answer, she put 'writer'. Then it asked what Carol did for relaxation, and she put down the truth—'writing'. The third question asked for her hobbies. Well, not wanting to look obsessed, she crossed her fingers and answered 'swimming'. But, given that the chlorine in the pool does terrible things to her highlights, I'm sure you can guess the real answer!

Books by Carol Marinelli

Mills & Boon Medical Romance

London's Most Desirable Docs
Unwrapping Her Italian Doc
Playing the Playboy's Sweetheart

Bayside Hospital Heartbreakers!
Tempted by Dr Morales
The Accidental Romeo

NYC Angels: Redeeming the Playboy
200 Harley Street: Surgeon in a Tux
Baby Twins to Bind Them
Just One Night?
The Baby of Their Dreams
The Socialite's Secret

Visit the Author Profile page at millsandboon.co.uk for more titles.

CHAPTER ONE

'YOU ALREADY KNOW, don't you, Freya?'

'Know what?' Freya frowned as she attempted to pull up the zipper on her friend Beth's wedding dress. It had slipped up easily at the final fitting just last week so Freya gave it another tug but it refused to budge. 'Have you...?'

Freya stopped herself from continuing with the question. She, more than most, knew just how much damage that a throwaway comment about weight could cause and she certainly didn't want to inflict that pain on Beth. Especially not on her wedding day, but, hell, the dress was tight.

Then it dawned on Freya why she was having so much trouble getting Beth into her wedding dress. Beth had declined Freya's offer of champagne as they prepared for her late afternoon wedding and the girls' night in at Freya's apartment last week had been a very tame affair.

Freya worked it out just a split second before her friend said it.

'I'm pregnant!'

Oh, Freya was very grateful for that split second because her eyes had screwed closed as yet another friend revealed their happy news, but by the time Beth had turned around, Freya had composed herself and was smiling.

'That's fantastic news, Beth.'

'Don't pretend that you didn't know.'

'I honestly had no idea,' Freya admitted.

'I didn't have even one of the cocktails you'd made!'

'I thought it was a bit odd,' Freya admitted, because Beth loved a drink. 'I just believed you when you said that you were detoxing for the wedding.'

Oh, it had been a tame night. Two of the women were pregnant, one was breastfeeding and now Freya understood why Beth had also declined the cocktails that Freya had prepared. For Freya, it had been a long night of being told, *It will be your turn soon,* and asked, *Are you still not seeing anyone?* Her friends didn't know about her fertility issues, so they hadn't been deliberately insensitive. She could have told them that day that she'd had blood work done and when Hilary was back from her trip she would be having some further tests to see if she might be a candidate for IVF through an egg donor.

Freya didn't really open up to anyone, though, not fully.

'So when did you find out?' Freya asked Beth.

'Two weeks ago. I was devastated at first, I have to admit.'

'Devastated?' Freya checked. She knew very well that Beth and Neil both wanted a family and so she wondered if they had found out that there was something wrong with the baby.

'Well, I was very upset,' Beth clarified. 'We've been saving up for the honeymoon for ages and had paid for all drinks to be included...' Beth rolled her eyes at the perceived inconvenience. 'I'm fine about it now.'

Fine!

Freya did her best not to dwell on that word.

Finally the zip was up and she arranged the huge bow on Beth's dress.

Freya knew that she overthought everything but, really, to use the word *fine* to describe the news that you were pregnant irked her!

'Have you told your parents?' Freya asked once she had unclenched her jaw.

'Not yet. Neil's going to reveal the news during the speeches, so we can capture everyone's expressions. Can you warn the cameraman?'

'Sure.'

'You won't forget?'

'I never forget,' Freya said. 'That's why you've got me planning your wedding, remember!'

Oh, Freya was on edge and trying not to be but Beth really was a bridezilla.

'Okay, done. Wow. You look amazing!' Freya said. 'Simply stunning.'

No one could ever tell when Freya was lying. It was why she was so successful in PR.

The dress that Beth had chosen was a long sheath of ivory tulle, tied in the middle with a huge satin bow.

Like an oddly wrapped parcel, Freya thought.

Worse, Beth had chosen similar for Freya to wear. Hers was knee-length, though, and the shade of Freya's dress was Antique White. Freya felt as if she was wearing an old teabag. Her brunette hair had been teased into curls and Beth had insisted on red lips for them both. The only saving grace was that the bow on Freya's dress was smaller.

They looked like two poodles who'd been badly clipped, Freya thought as she stared at their reflections.

'Are you wearing a bra?' Beth checked.

'It didn't work with the dress,' Freya said.

'Well, put some plasters on them,' Beth said. 'I don't want *your* nipples in *my* photos.'

There was a knock at the door and, of course, brides didn't answer doors, so Freya opened it and smiled when she saw Beth's father, realising it was time for her to head down and check the last-minute details.

'Right, I'm going to go down and make sure everything is in place,' Freya said. 'Enjoy every moment and leave all the worrying to me.'

'I shall.' Beth nodded. 'It's all set for midnight?'

'It is.'

'I want everyone watching us kiss as we ring in the New Year.'

'They shall be.'

'Thanks for organising everything.'

'Well, it's been a lot more fun sorting out flowers and table plans than getting everyone at The Hills to glam up for the new brochure...'

'They're already a glam lot.'

'I know they are.' That hadn't been what Freya had meant but there wasn't time for all that now. 'I'll see you down in the hotel chapel.'

'Don't forget the plasters,' Beth reminded her. Freya smiled and picked up her posy of red flowers to match her red lips then stepped out of the room and let out a very long breath.

Again she had lied. This wedding had been *hell* to organise.

Two of the hotels that Beth and Neil had chosen as potential venues had explained that their stairways and escalators were for all of their guests, especially on New Year's Eve. It had been difficult to find somewhere to accommodate all their demands but Freya had achieved it.

The wedding was at five, then dinner and speeches, but instead of being able to relax afterwards she had to keep the cameraman and photographer sober, as well as get two hundred guests out of the ballroom and onto the main staircase. Oh, and her ex, Edward, was going to be there.

As he had been at three other weddings she'd attended this year.

Freya was so over weddings!

She knew that her PR skills were a very large reason that Beth had chosen her to be bridesmaid.

It didn't offend Freya.

To survive as top PR consultant in LA, you needed to keep in with your contacts. Beth was a journalist, and the many hours that Freya had spent organising the wedding would be returned in kind.

It was called networking and Freya was very good at that.

Freya got to her hotel room to freshen up. She checked her make-up and wished she hadn't—it was far too much.

She really didn't like this dress and how *much*

it revealed of her shoulders. Her upper back was bare too and she felt exposed. Freya turned and craned her neck and told herself that everyone in the chapel would be looking at the bride rather than the bridesmaid's spinal column.

As always, she checked her phone and saw that there were several messages and missed calls from her brother, James.

Work.

Freya knew that it would be.

James Rothsberg was *the* cosmetic surgeon in LA and for the past six years he had poured everything into The Hollywood Hills Medical Center. It was an amazing facility frequented by the rich and famous. Affectionately known as The Hills, it had everything from obstetrics to intensive care and was the top tier of health care. Two years ago James had asked Freya to come on board and she had put her PR skills to excellent commercial use.

Till now.

It was time to give back, she had told James.

And he'd listened.

Which was why, instead of rolling her eyes at

being called late afternoon on New Year's Eve, Freya called her brother.

'Hi, James,' Freya said. 'You've been trying to get hold of me.'

'I have,' James said. 'Freya, I need you at The Hills tomorrow at nine.'

'On New Year's Day?' Freya checked.

'I've just taken a call from Geoff, and Paulo's condition has deteriorated. I've just spoken with Zackary and he's agreed to come in and be interviewed tomorrow instead of waiting till Monday.'

Freya's eyes screwed closed as James carried on talking.

'I need you to be at the interview.'

'Me?' Freya tried to keep the quake from her voice. 'Since when did I sit in on the hiring of medical personnel?'

'Since you talked me into taking on charitable cases,' James answered tartly. 'And, given we're going to be asking him to donate his skills for nothing...'

'He already knows that he'll be doing some pro bono work.'

'Freya?'

She could hear the question in her brother's voice at her reluctance to sit in on the interview. After all, Freya had been the one pushing for The Hills to embrace this. Freya had been the one looking into a suitable charity to properly support and now things were finally moving along. But what James didn't understand was that the very seemingly together, always-very-much-in-control Freya had got herself into a little pickle that her older brother didn't know about.

There was a big pickle her brother didn't know about either, namely that the charity she'd found was headed by his ex, Mila Brightman, but it was the other pickle in the jar that Freya was wrestling with now.

She had already been dreading meeting the hot-shot cardiac surgeon Zackary Carlton.

Or Zack, as she'd found out he'd prefer to be known.

They had flirted via emails.

Not much.

It felt massive to Freya, though.

'I need you there tomorrow at nine,' James said. 'I'm sure he's going to have questions about the promotional side of things and I want a press release out saying that we have Zackary on board.'

'Zack!' Freya said. 'He prefers to be called Zack.'

'Noted,' James responded. 'I'll see you tomorrow at nine. I'll flick over some details tonight.'

'Thanks.'

Oh, God.

After the tame girls' night with her smug married friends, Freya had poured another cocktail and opened up her laptop and located a certain series of emails.

She never got involved with people she worked with. Actually, Freya really didn't get too involved full stop. But this teeny tiny flirt had been fun and Zack had outright asked if she was single.

Several daiquiris later, when Freya, who took her health seriously and didn't often drink, had decided to embrace the merits of *not* being married, she had typed her response back.

Very single. (Don't tell James.)

And now, tomorrow, she had to face him.

His response had made her blush and it was making her blush now.

I never kiss and tell.

Hopefully he wouldn't get the role, Freya thought, but who was she kidding? James wanted Zack Carlton on board, so much so that he had him currently housed in a luxury apartment that The Hills owned and was interviewing him on New Year's Day.

It had been a stupid flirt, a tiny one, but it had been completely out of character for her, and not just professionally. Freya wasn't a flirty person at all, she was far too controlled for that.

Blame it on the daiquiris.

Actually, she couldn't because the flirt had started a couple of emails prior to that.

She sighed. He was probably fifty and married with sixteen children. She'd blush about it tomorrow, but right now she had to deal with the wedding.

First, though, she texted her neighbour Red.

Freya had a late checkout but hadn't been intending to use it as she wanted to get home to her little dog, Cleo. Instead, she asked Red if he would let her out and feed her in the morning.

With that sorted she went to go but then Freya caught sight of her bare shoulders; she turned and looked again at her spine.

It had been that sight that had terrified James. Freya could still remember his shocked reaction as he had sat her up so that the doctor could listen to her chest.

'Freya!'

She had always kept this part of her body covered, hiding her secret, denying to everyone she had a problem, partying her way through her parents' appalling divorce and pretending she didn't care.

It was hard enough having high-profile actors as parents and wearing the Rothsberg name, but when that marriage had ended, to have it played out over the media had been agony.

And when a journalist had pointed out that Freya was just a little bit younger than her father's latest girlfriend, a magazine had taken it one nasty step further and pointed out that Freya was also considerably larger.

Her comfort during the very public break-up had, till then, been food and she'd had to endure the spotlight that had shone on her parents suddenly widening to accommodate both herself and James.

She had rigorously denied herself the comfort of food.

Very rigorously!

And she had also partied hard.

James had hauled her out of a nightclub and, too weak to row with her brother, Freya had collapsed and been rushed to hospital.

There she had been stripped and put into a gown and then James had been allowed back in, and that was when he had seen her spine and the true extent of her problem had been exposed.

Now, fourteen years later, she would stand today with the most loathed part of her body on show and, joy of joys, eat at the top table.

Freya was better now—so, so much better.

Recovered, healed, whatever the best word was, but there were still hurts and repercussions that she had to deal with, and one of the big ones was that she rarely had a period.

Seriously rarely.

Once, maybe twice a year.

'It's your own fault,' Freya told her reflection, and then came away from the mirror and headed out to the elevator.

She got in and closed her eyes, resting against the wall as she angled her neck to release tension. When she opened them, instead of being on the mezzanine level, she was on the ground floor, and looking into the eyes of Him!

'Well, you prove my theory,' he said in a deep, sexy voice.

It was Him!

The man she had seen a few days ago.

Freya had been speaking with the hotel's events coordinator and working out how long they would need to freeze the escalators for, when they'd both stopped talking as the sound of Cuban heels had rung out on the marble floor. And they had stopped talking with good reason. Tall, tanned, with shaggy, curly black hair, he had walked past them in dark jeans and tight T-shirt, carrying a

large backpack. He had been just so sexy that
he'd simply stopped conversations. Both women
had watched him go up to the desk to check in
and then shared a guilty smile once they'd finished checking him out.

And now Freya was in the lift with Him.

'And your theory is?' Freya asked.

'That all the good girls are taken.' He asked her
which floor she wanted. 'I've already pressed...'
Actually, no, her selection had been erased. 'The
mezzanine level.' She watched as long suntanned
fingers pressed said level and then he pressed
for floor twenty-eight and she wished, how she
wished, she had given the thirtieth floor as her
choice of destination, just for a minute or two
more alone with him.

'Shouldn't brides be smiling on their wedding
day?' he asked, and Freya tried to place his accent.

'Believe me, the bride is smiling,' Freya said
in a dry voice. 'I'm the bridesmaid.'

'Did I hear the word *maid*?'

Freya laughed at the cheeky inference and the
slow smile he gave in return had her stomach

tighten. Sexy green eyes were looking right at her, and he didn't make her feel like an old maid in the least...

Freya blinked at her own thought process.

The hotel events coordinator had, when they'd been watching him, sighed that he was probably gay and Freya had said if that were the case, *again*, then she really had to get out of LA.

Oh, he was so not gay. His eyes might as well be blowtorches because he had her face just turn to fire.

Sadly the doors pinged open.

'Enjoy the wedding...' he said.

'Oh, I shan't, it's going to be a very long evening,' Freya replied, peeling herself from the wall, when she really didn't want to get out.

'Yeah, I get it.' he said. 'I do my best to avoid weddings.' He met her eyes. 'Especially my own.'

Was he telling her that he was single?

She thought back to the flirty emails that she would live to regret tomorrow, but flirting was kind of fun, Freya was finding out, and she was *very* single.

'And me,' Freya said.

The elevator doors were open but the conversation wasn't closed and he put one big boot out to keep them open as he asked Freya a question. 'Why did she want a big white wedding on a Thursday?'

'Because it's New Year's Eve.'

'So it is! Well, thanks for reminding me, I'd be in trouble if I didn't call home.'

'You're Australian?' Freya asked, now that she'd placed his accent.

He nodded.

'LA's a long way from home.'

'It is,' he answered. 'And I'm suddenly lonely.'

He didn't look lonely in the least, not with that smile.

'Poor you,' Freya replied, and met his smouldering gaze. His deep green eyes were thickly lashed and she looked down to a dark red mouth and stubbled jaw.

He was so hot, so direct, so bad, so sexy and her reaction to him so acute that Freya could possibly have forgiven herself if she'd hit the button to close the doors and leapt up onto those lean hips.

'I'd better go,' she said, because, yes, she'd better. 'It was nice to meet you…' Freya fished for his name.

'We don't need names, do we?'

She ought to have been offended, Freya thought. She ought to be very, very offended and yet she wasn't.

'Enjoy the wedding,' he offered, 'and thanks for messing up my theory.'

'But I haven't,' Freya said, simply unable to resist prolonging this delicious, rare flirt and, just as when she had hit 'send' on that blasted email, she offered a verbal response that would be just as hard to retract. 'I'm not a good girl.'

'It would seem that you are,' he answered smoothly, 'given that you're about to get out.'

The bow around her middle was killing Freya. She wanted to tear it off, and the dress too, and stamp on them. Instead she stood as his eyes performed a long and slow perusal of her aroused body and Beth would be furious because her nipples were throbbing. They needed his mouth. Oh, yes, they did.

Oh, she was in no position to take offence as his

gaze lingered and lingered, because Freya was doing the exact same thing to him. Down that wide chest her eyes went. He was wearing a silver-grey T-shirt and he too had two nipples, she knew that because she counted them slowly and carefully. Then she looked down to his flat stomach. His T-shirt was half-tucked in and she fought not to lift it free. He had on a heavy leather belt that made her thighs want to press together. She looked at the thick bulge in his jeans and was frustrated by the button-up flies, because she'd break her nails tearing at them just to get to him. What the hell was happening? Freya wondered. Because she completely wanted to sink to her knees and to do just that.

It was, for Freya, the oddest feeling. She wasn't very free in bed and she wasn't the most generous lover. She just hoped to have her needs met. 'One for you, one for me' type of thing, and if her needs weren't met then she'd lie twitching with resentment. Actually, even if they were met, it was so underwhelming that she lay twitching anyway, wondering why she couldn't enjoy it. Freya controlled everything that went in her mouth and what she was looking at now wasn't one of them.

Freya licked her lips, not deliberately but very provocatively, it would seem, because he just grew before her eyes. She watched as that lovely hand that had earlier pressed the button had no choice but to make a little room and he rearranged himself to her eyes.

Freya tore them from his bulging crotch and he gave her a slow, appreciative smile in reward for her lovely effort to get him so hard and so soon.

'I'm impressed,' he said.

'With what?' Freya breathed. She could hardly speak.

'It takes great skill to be such a turn-on in that dress.'

And Freya had more than seen just how turned on he was. 'I have to go.'

'Then go.'

He didn't remove his boot from the door, and Freya could either step over his leg or walk around him. The scent of him mingled with her arousal and Freya had this terrifying moment of absolute conviction that she wasn't going to make it to the chapel in time.

He was sex.

And suddenly, for the first time in her life, so was she.

Freya didn't walk around him, she put one high-heeled foot over his calf and proceeded to step over the hurdle.

She'd never gotten over them at school and was having the same trouble now.

He was terribly polite, for such a filthy animal he really was extremely polite, because his hand settled on her arm to help her over.

Oh, she needed help because the feel of his warm fingers on her bare skin had Freya wanting to straddle his calf and she knew that the bastard knew it.

'Do you want to come up for a drink?' he offered in that low, sexy, deep voice but, really, why bother attempting to be polite? Freya thought. A drink was the very last thing on either of their minds.

'I have a wedding to get to,' Freya croaked. 'I really do.'

'Then you'd better go, or you're going to be extremely unpresentable very soon.'

Oh, those eyes, Freya thought, unwilling to leave the heat of his gaze, but then she looked at his mouth as he stated what he'd already achieved.

'I want to mess you up,' he said. 'I want you dishevelled.'

She deserved a gold medal and the national anthem sung in her honour because she had made it over his leg. Freya tried to walk off, she really did, but her muscles were protesting and her damp knickers were demanding that she take them off.

'Hey,' he called to her blushing shoulders. She could feel his eyes on her spine and it didn't make her feel ill, instead it made Freya, foolishly, dangerously, turn around. 'If the wedding gets to be a bit…' He shrugged. And then, with utter and no doubt practised ease, he gave her a free pass to heaven. 'Room 2812.'

CHAPTER TWO

'FREYA?' THE HOTEL'S events coordinator prompted when Freya didn't answer her question.

'I was just taking it all in,' Freya said, rather than admit her mind was still back in the elevator. She looked around the ballroom. 'Yes, Beth's going to be very pleased.'

The tables were dressed in red but instead of having flowers as centrepieces Beth had decided on huge bows. There were bows on the chairs too. Freya's carefully worded response told the hotel events coordinator that she had done an amazing job with terrible directions.

They shared another small smile and Freya nearly burst out laughing, a part of her wanting to tell the other woman about her little...er...encounter with the man they'd been admiring a few days ago. Instead, she headed off to the chapel where guests were starting to arrive, hugging the memory to herself and smiling. It had been fun and Freya had never had fun like that.

Freya knew that she was a private, prickly person.

She was, thanks to her psychology degree that lay languishing unused on her résumé, very self-aware. And her very self-aware self knew why she didn't let her guard down.

Freya didn't trust anyone with her feelings.

And walking towards her was yet another reason why.

Edward!

'Freya, we have to stop meeting like this.' He smiled.

'Well, now that all our friends are married, we shall,' Freya answered coolly.

'Won't I be getting an invite to yours?' Edward asked.

'That would be a no,' Freya said.

'Are you here with anyone?'

Freya was not going to prolong this conversation so she gave him a very tight smile and walked off.

Oh, how she loathed him.

He was married now and had twins but that hadn't stopped him from trying to chat her up at the last wedding they'd been at. Freya knew, because she'd been dealing with the RSVPs, that Cathy, his wife, wasn't attending tonight as one of their children was unwell.

Oh, a come-on from Edward she so did not need.

Not when she had Mr Room 2812, Freya thought with a sudden smile.

Of course she wouldn't be taking him up on his offer but it had been such, *such* a nice offer to have that it got her through the wedding and then the meal.

The endless five-course meal at the top table.

It was hard to explain, even to herself, but set menus were for Freya the hardest.

Chicken or beef was served alternatively and Freya let out a small breath of relief that she was given chicken, which would have been her choice.

'Would you mind...?' Beth's mother said. 'I don't like red meat.'

'Of course.' Freya smiled, to show that it didn't matter in the least to her, and they swapped plates.

She had been worried about the meal at the wedding and had thought about talking to her friend, Mila, about it. She sometimes discussed her eating disorder with Mila, because Mila didn't treat Freya as if she had two heads and tiptoe around her. But weddings were a bit of a touchy subject between Freya and Mila, given James had jilted her friend at the altar. Also, she was avoiding Mila a bit at the moment, because Freya still hadn't told James that the Bright Hope Clinic charity was run by his ex-fiancée.

James didn't even know they'd remained friends.

Oh, it was a long dinner and then came the speeches.

Freya glared at the cameraman, who was getting stuck into the champagne. She would have preferred Beth to have chosen someone else, but the wedding budget was getting tight, Beth had said. Freya had gently suggested losing a few bows but that hadn't gone down well.

'My wife and I have an extra surprise for you

all,' Neil said. 'You'll be thrilled to know that the stork arrived early...'

The whole room melted and clapped and the cameraman must have seen Freya's stern glare because he panned to the guests and then back to the happy couple. Neil made a joke about more free cocktails for him on their cruise. This had Freya's jaw tense.

Then the dancing started but Freya still couldn't relax as Beth had yet more requests.

'I want him to film messages for us from all the guests.'

'I know that you do.'

'But I don't want the messages to just be about the baby,' Beth said. 'I want them mainly to be about me.'

Me, me, me, me, me, Freya thought as she nodded and smiled.

Freya took a glass of champagne from a passing waiter and then Edward came over. 'You're looking gorgeous, Freya,' he said.

She looked terrible, as Mr Room 2812 had so sexily pointed out!

'Can I get you another drink?' Edward offered.

'No, thank you.'

'You were blonde last time I saw you,' he said. 'You've gone back to brunette.'

'Really?' Freya's response was sarcastic. 'Thanks for letting me know.'

'I'm actually staying here tonight,' Edward said. 'How about a dance for old times' sake?'

'How about I throw this champagne in your face?'

Freya walked off with her drink and headed outside to drag the cool night air into her lungs. She loved LA in winter and she promised to take herself riding some time soon. It was her best method for relaxing and she had been introduced to it when she had been in rehab.

Freya never cried.

Not even in rehab had she let them break her but tonight she suddenly felt close.

It wasn't Edward, she harboured no hidden feelings for him—well, no nice ones.

It was how they'd ended things that still stung, all these years on.

Her long stint in rehab had been spread far and wide across the media and everyone had thought she'd been on drugs. At the age of twenty-three, when they'd started dating, he'd asked about it and Freya had told him about her eating disorder.

It had been hard to reveal but she'd pushed on and had told him she was recovered, or healed, or whatever the best word was. But when she'd told him that she probably couldn't have children he had, on the spot, dumped her and accused her of stringing him along. It had felt as if Edward had only been dating her on the assumption that one day she'd be pregnant.

'I thought we were enjoying each other's company,' Freya had said. 'Not looking for future mating partners.'

'Well, it's preferable to have that option,' had been his callous response.

It had hurt, it had been such a horrible blow to her recovering self, but she had refused to let it plunge her back into hell.

Freya knew she should go back inside but she could not face Edward.

Did he think she'd have an affair, that married

men were all that was left? Oh, no, she would
rather, far rather, get in that elevator and…

Why not? Freya thought.

They'd both, in that brief exchange, stated that
they were single.

And she'd promised this coming year to do
more of the things she liked and to try new things.

No.

Freya simply couldn't see it.

Going up and knocking on Sexy Bastard's door
just for sex.

Or maybe he'd left it open and she would just
slip in.

Actually, Freya could see it.

And she *had* promised to keep her New Year's
resolutions…

New Year.

Yikes! Freya remembered a little too late that
she had to get everyone out for the photo shoot
and the next twenty minutes were frantic indeed.

It had been a long and difficult night, Freya
thought, and a part of her longed to just head upstairs and to find out what simply letting go and
having fun actually meant.

* * *

An aching part of Zack had really wished she would head up!

He'd arrived back in his room so turned on and waiting.

Come on, he'd thought.

God knew, he'd needed the distraction.

He'd unlatched the door and lain on the bed, hands behind his head.

She was stunning.

Dark eyes, dark hair and that mouth… She'd looked a little familiar but all he had ever seen of LA till now had been the airport so Zack had shrugged that thought off. It would come to him overnight.

Would she?

Of course she would. The attraction had been through the roof but by ten he'd downgraded his expectations because the speeches were surely well over with.

By eleven-thirty he'd woken from a doze and stared out to the LA night.

Not at the city but at the mountains beyond and he knew he had to ring his parents before the lines got busy. He got up and took out his cellphone and took a steadying breath before he made the call.

Zack was thirty-three and the last time he'd been home, a couple of years ago, he'd been the same age as his brother Toby had been when he had died.

Except Toby had been married and working in the family practice and his wife, Alice, had wanted to start a family.

Whereas Zack, as his parents had constantly pointed out, was a drifter.

He was a highly skilled paediatric cardiac surgeon, Zack had riposted, but that was just boasting, he was told. And what good were his skills when they were so badly needed in Kurranda, the remote outback town where he and Toby had been raised.

He could picture the phone ringing in the hall. Reception was haphazard there and the landline to the family doctor really was a lifeline for the community.

His mother answered on the third ring.

'Hey, Mum,' Zack said. 'Happy New Year.'

'I'm sure it is where you are.'

Zack closed his eyes, it was just more of the same.

'How's Nepal?'

'I'm in LA,' Zack answered.

'I thought you *had* to be in Nepal.'

'I did have to be there for Christmas,' Zack answered. 'There was an operation I wanted to do before I left but we had to wait for some equipment to arrive. I would have been home if I could.'

'Well, why aren't you now?'

'Because I've got an interview tomorrow.'

'In LA?'

'It's a top medical centre. They've got some of the most amazing equipment and facilities and I don't want to let that side of things slide…' Zack stopped even attempting to explain. He did not want to argue with his mother. Judy Carlton simply could not, would not, get it, and Zack was over trying to explain. 'Is Dad there?'

'You just missed him. He got called out for Tara. Do you remember her?'

Of course he damn well remembered, they'd

been friends. What his mother didn't know was
that they had been each other's first. Zack had
fought to stop that getting out as Tara's father
was very religious.

Zack stayed silent.

'She married Jed.'

'Yep.'

'Well, the baby's not due till the end of January but it looks as if she might deliver early and
it's breech. I can't talk for long, they might need
the air ambulance...'

'I get it.' Zack said. 'Will you wish Dad a happy
New Year for me and could you—?'

'Zack,' his mum broke in, 'you should be here
to say it to him for yourself. Even if you'd just
come home on a stopover it would have been
something.'

'I would have but this interview is being slotted
in, they need me to start straight away. There's a
very sick child—'

'Oh, I don't have time for your fancy position,'
Judy said. 'I'll pass on to Tara and her husband
how well you're doing, shall I?'

Zack knew that translated to, *You should be*

back here, scrubbing in with your father, rather than Tara having to be airlifted. 'That was a low blow.'

'I know.' His mother didn't quite apologise. 'I'm tired, Zack, and your dad is too. He didn't get any break over Christmas and the place just seems to be getting busier. So much for retiring.'

Zack closed his eyes. Sometimes he wished he could just give up on his own dreams and give them the solution they wanted.

'By now you and Toby...' Judy swallowed and Zack then heard his mother, a very strong woman, give way to tears. New Year always did that to her and this coming year marked another difficult milestone. 'It will be ten years soon.'

'I know it will.'

At the beginning of February it would be ten years since Toby had died.

He and Zack had been on a weekend away. Both had been good horsemen but a snake had spooked Toby's horse and thrown him off.

Zack looked out of the hotel window again and out towards the dark shadows of the hills and thought of the red earth of home. Even if he didn't want to be there for ever he missed it at times and now was one of those times. As he stood there he remembered too the agony of hours spent with his brother, waiting for help to arrive while knowing there was none to be had.

At the age of thirty-one Toby had died in his younger brother's arms.

Zack knew his mother needed to talk and so he forgot about the sniping and let her.

'Things would be so different if he was still alive. He loved the clinic. Toby and your father had such plans for it. Alice is pregnant again by her new husband.'

He was hardly her new husband, Zack thought. Alice had been remarried for seven years.

'Mum, she's allowed to be happy.'

'She and Toby were so happy, though,' Judy said. 'I wanted grandchildren.'

'I know.'

'And that's not going to happen, is it?'

'No.'

'Are you seeing someone?'

She asked him the same question every time

they spoke and it was always the same answer he gave. 'No one serious.'

'Zack…?'

'What?' Zack said, and when there was silence he told her the truth. 'Mum, I won't be giving you grandchildren.'

Zack was direct, yes. There was no point giving her false hope. The life his parents had planned for him wasn't the one he wanted. He never wanted to be tied down, not to one person and not to one place.

Zack wasn't cruel, though.

What he didn't tell his mother was that Toby had been far from happy with his life.

That was the reason Toby had called him up and asked if he'd join him on a weekend away. There, in the outback, lying by a fire, looking up at the stars, Toby had told him the truth—that he felt stifled, and wanted away, not just from Kurranda and the medical practice but also from his marriage.

Zack had been stunned. He'd thought that Alice and Toby, childhood sweethearts, had been so happy but Toby had told him that, no, things hadn't been good for a very long while.

It had been a long night spent talking, sometimes seriously, but also they'd shared laughter, not knowing what was to come the very next day.

Toby hadn't quite taken that secret to his grave, it had been left with Zack. He'd never shared it with anyone and it weighed heavily inside.

'I really do have to go,' Judy said. 'I'd better head over there now in case your dad needs help to organise the air ambulance and things…' His mother wasn't a doctor or nurse but she was a huge part of the fabric of the town. She would liaise with the air ambulance and locals and make sure the transfer was seamless. Then she'd have Tara's parents over for coffee and a meal as they awaited news.

That was who his mother was.

'Happy New Year,' Zack said.

Judy made a small huffing noise.

His parents had decided, on Toby's death and Zack's failure to settle, that there could be no more happy years.

'Happy New Year, Zack,' Judy said, but even

that came out with a slight edge. Zack made sure he was happy, that he lived, that he grabbed this rare gift by the throat and got every bit of life out of it.

He'd promised his brother he would.

'Mum,' Zack suddenly said. 'I'll come home for a visit in April. Tell Dad that.'

'For how long?'

'I'm not sure, but I'll be back to see you both then.'

He ended the call and though he could not stand the thought of living back there, and being in a place where everyone knew your business, it didn't mean he didn't love nature and space and the people.

And, though things were strained, he loved his family.

Zack lay on the bed and closed his eyes but he couldn't unwind. Speaking with his parents always left him feeling like that. The plans his parents had had for him had been set in stone from the day he was born. They just hadn't thought to consult the baby they had made.

He was to study medicine in Melbourne as his

father and brother had done, but even before he had left for the city Zack had known in his heart that he wasn't coming back.

Tara had known it too.

Of course he remembered Tara.

Not just the hot, sexy kisses behind a barn and sultry outback nights, more he remembered a conversation that had taken place the night before he'd left as they'd lain in each other's arms.

'You're not coming back, are you?' Tara had asked.

'You talk as if I'm leaving the country. I'm only going to Melbourne. I'll be back for the summer breaks.' Even at eighteen he'd been direct. 'But, no, I can't see myself here, Tara.'

'And I don't want to be there,' Tara said. She was a country girl and loved it and neither wanted to change or to change the other.

'Have you told your parents?' she asked.

'I've tried,' Zack said. 'They don't understand.'

He was still trying.

And all these years later they still didn't understand.

Zack went to pour a drink but the half-bottle

of wine was empty and he wasn't a big fan of American beer.

He was about to ring for room service but, still churned up from the conversation with his mother, he pulled on his boots again and took the elevator down, but it only took him to the mezzanine level and he decided to take the escalator down to the bar.

There were people everywhere, all standing on the stairs, and then he found out why.

The wedding.

'You'll have to use the elevators if you want to get to the ground floor,' someone told him, and they sounded annoyed. 'The escalators and stairs are in use.'

And there was the woman from said elevator, organising the wedding party, telling people to step back or to stand a fraction more to the left.

Zack watched as a gentleman came over to her and whatever she said had him step abruptly back.

Oh, she was a snappy, bossy little thing, Zack thought.

Not with him, though.

And then she looked up.

Oh, my... Freya thought, and another of Edward's sleazy come-ons left her mind.

If Mr 2812 had been sexy before, he was sinfully so now—dishevelled and just raw male, he made her toes curl in her very painful shoes. His hair was messy, his T-shirt was all crumpled and, alongside all the suits and formal clothes, in those dark jeans and tight T-shirt he stood out, deliciously so.

Freya dragged her mind away from rude thoughts. This shot was important and the countdown had started. Beth and Neil were in position and everyone was in place and she should be able to relax soon. All she had to do was wave the happy couple off and the rest of the night was hers.

Concentrate, Freya.

She couldn't.

There was just this prickling awareness all over her as she recalled his scent and the feel of his hand on her arm.

Oh, God. She gazed up at him and hoped her

eyes weren't frantic, but that was how she suddenly felt—frantic for him.

'Ten!' everybody shouted. 'Nine!'

They could not stop staring and, as the countdown drew to its conclusion, as everyone started cheering and kissing, Beth's carefully organised photos were ruined by a tall guy bursting through and dashing down the stairs.

'Auld Lang Syne' was being sung out around them as his hands took her by the upper arms. Briefly she wondered why, instead of kissing her as she badly needed him to do, he was moving her away. But then Freya found out exactly why.

This wasn't a kiss suitable for public exposure.

They were in a small booth to the side of the hotel's reception when his mouth first met hers. They came together so hard that their teeth met and his tongue was strong and thick and very indecent. Her hips were held by him, and animal passion, which had never taken up residence in Freya before, rapidly made itself right at home.

Her hands were pressing into his chest, not to push him away, just to feel him, to rub those solid muscles beneath greedy palms. Then they went up to his head and her fingers dug into his hair. She kissed him back on tiptoe, so that her heels lifted up out of her shoes in an attempt to scale him.

He pulled back and gave her an intense look and there was no mention of going up for a drink.

'I have to get back...' It was a feeble protest she made. 'I just need ten more minutes to sort the wedding party out.'

'We can't wait.'

His erection was in her groin and Freya herself was pressing hard into him.

'I have to make sure that they get off okay...'

He peered out.

'They're waving and the bride is about to throw the bouquet. Do you want to go and try to catch it?'

The question was a loaded one.

What was she looking for—an amazing night with no names, or to dash off and catch the bouquet and the dream that it might one day be her?

'God, no,' Freya said. She was more than happy with being a third-time bridesmaid and so she took his head in her hands and got back to that mouth for one more deep kiss before they hit the elevators.

Freya pressed the button for the twenty-eighth floor.

'You remembered,' he said.

'Oh, yes!'

CHAPTER THREE

SADLY FOR THEM the elevator was full.

The wedding guests were dispersing and either heading to their rooms or to the bars. There were many, many opportunities for Freya to change her mind on the long and frustrating ride to the twenty-eighth floor and say that this was a terrible idea and so not like her.

It never entered Freya's head to do so.

Her rigid, controlled life was in desperate need of fun and adventure, and he offered that and more.

He was beautiful.

Even with her back to him she could feel the energy between them, it was utter attraction and arousal at its most basic and Freya could not wait to indulge.

'What floor are you on?' he asked, running a

finger over her bare shoulder as they crawled towards her floor. His touch was electric and, yes,
it was terribly tempting to get off at the tenth
floor, but there might be a problem as she hadn't
packed her toiletry bag with a wild night in mind.

She gave a small shake of her head and then
turned and looked him right in the eye as the elevator came to her floor and a couple got out.

'I haven't got…' she mouthed.

'I have,' he mouthed back. Of course he did,
Freya thought. This guy had nearly had her at
five p.m. after all—no doubt he came prepared
for women dropping their knickers on sight—
but they were already past her floor and so they
waited—oh, how they waited—for them to hit
his floor.

As the crowd thinned out there was a bit more
space but they didn't utilise it. She could feel his
eyes on her shoulder, on her spine, and then she
got the bliss of his mouth on the part of her she
hated the most.

She leant back into him even as the doors
opened.

'Thank God,' Zack said, and he took her hand and they just about ran the length of the corridor.

He opened up the door and they fell into the room. Their mouths locked and they didn't bother with the lights. Just hot, hard kisses as Freya kissed him with abandon up against the wall.

He more than partook because he tore that dress off and the sound of it ripping was as delicious as the feel of his hands on her bare skin.

'Oh, God,' he said as he played with her breasts and tweaked her nipples as if he'd been waiting for them all night.

He had been.

Freya had never been more grateful for ignoring the bride's plea because, unable to resist a taste, he lowered his head and took one nipple into his hungry mouth.

'She wanted me to wear sticking plasters over them.'

'We don't like the bride,' he said as he withdrew his mouth, and it made her laugh. It was just such a relief after a very long and difficult day to laugh and vent to someone who got her.

He took the other breast in his mouth and sucked hard. Freya pushed him off, only because it was her turn to taste *his* salty chest. Oh, he tasted amazing, like he'd been swimming in the ocean and had then showered in ice. Salty, refreshing and so firm.

Freya dealt with his heavy leather belt as best she could with her mouth on his chest, licking him, tasting him and then moaning her frustration.

'Why button-ups...?' Freya whimpered.

'So I can picture your fingers undoing them and getting it out.' She was doing just that and Freya herself wasn't gentle. He was so thick and long and already there was a silver drizzle that trickled onto her fingers as she explored him.

'Get naked,' he told her, and he went into his pocket. He wished he'd kicked off his boots so he could do the same but there really wasn't time. As she shed her knickers he dressed his erection and Freya toppled a little as she took off her shoes.

'Come here,' he said, and she just stepped to him and he lifted her to where she'd wanted to be all along.

'Oh…' He didn't guide her on, he held her hips as her hands went behind his neck.

'Lean back,' he told her, and as he held her by the hips he rubbed her wet sex over his stomach and scented himself with her.

'I'm going to come…' Freya was, the feel of the hairs on his stomach, the rough guide of his hands, the way he was holding her, and she couldn't hold on.

'That's the intention,' Sexy Bastard said.

She had kind of got this wasn't going to be like anything she'd experienced before but she found out for certain then. As her body arched, as she let out a building moan, he took her coming. He just drove into her tight and twitching and moaned at the pleasure.

'Oh, yeah,' he said.

Oh, yes, Freya thought.

He just parted her orgasm, it was like being a virgin all over again, or not, Freya thought because that had been *such* an underwhelming encounter.

This wasn't.

She went limp for a moment and he took full

advantage, grinding her down to meet his thrusts. Her hands took in his muscled shoulders and she dug her nails in, and then she just had to taste that shoulder, sucking it as her hands explored his broad upper back.

Her nails dug in again, deeper, and he took her a bit slower but with measured tension. It was an odd consent but she read it—he wanted more of the same so she scratched him hard.

'Careful,' he warned as her mouth sucked skin, but he wasn't telling her to stop, she knew that. 'You'll pay for each bruise.'

Oh, she would gladly pay.

He took her to the desk, or she guessed that's what it was, because it was cold and hard on her back. Freya went to wrap her legs around him but his hand pressed her thighs apart and he took her hard and so deep that she just about performed a sit-up as her entire lower abdomen contracted.

'Come on,' he said, and she opened her eyes to his gruff command but then her eyes met his and he smiled down at her.

'Nice,' he said, bucking into her.

'So…' Freya couldn't finish. She had never known anything like it. His face tensed and then he released into her, and she met the impact with a deep force of her own. Her orgasm just rolled through her like thunder and then lightning clapped her tight with no pause in between. It just dissolved her from the inside out, and as it left she quivered and then he collapsed onto her.

He was so heavy, and breathless, but then his mouth was an unexpected soft caress. Even as he came out of her he kissed her. Even as he unsheathed he kissed her back to earth, and as he stripped off his boots and jeans, his mouth never left her skin. Naked now, he picked her up from the hard desk and carried her to the bed.

He got in beside her and scooped her into his body. His hand stroked her breast and he kissed her shoulder as she lay feeling bewildered yet drowsy and sedated.

'Go to sleep,' he said.

He seemed to know just what she needed and yet they didn't even know each other's names.

'How…?' She attempted to gather a thought into a sentence.

'Chemistry,' he answered.

And to sleep they went.

CHAPTER FOUR

'I SHOULD HAVE paid way more attention in science class,' Freya said a few hours later as she woke to the thought of his last word and the feel of her loose, relaxed body in his arms as he spooned in behind her.

'Oh, I'll make you pay attention,' he said low and deep into her ear. 'Happy New Year.'

'And you,' Freya said.

'It already is.'

Last night he'd barely been able to get the words out to his mother, knowing how pointless they were, but now Zack was happy, indulging in one of his passions.

The other was work and that was so intense that he lived for escapes like this.

'Were you going to come to my room?' he asked. 'Honest answer.'

'I was thinking about it,' Freya said. 'I wasn't having the best night.'

'What did you say to that guy?'

Freya frowned.

'The one who walked off just before you saw me...'

'Oh, that was Edward—'

'No names,' he interrupted, and Freya lay there, feeling his fingers gently kneading her stomach.

Freya wanted to know his name, she wanted to know more about him, and yet he'd reminded her that there would be no exchange of names. But as she lay there, enjoying the gentle massage of his fingers, and thought about it, she realised that it was actually quite freeing. There would be no *I'm Freya Rothsberg. Yes, Aubrey St Claire and Michael Rothsberg are indeed my parents.* And if he recognised the name, then he'd know about their messy divorce. And there would be no *I'm thirty-one, single, perfectionist, infertile but trying not to be, recovered anorexic.* She didn't have to say she was a big shot in PR. Or that she was stressing about taking on the charity side of her brother's medical centre. Or that, though she'd pushed James to let her, really she wanted to use her psychology degree.

No names didn't mean no past but it meant she didn't have to reveal anything that she didn't want to.

Who was she without all of that? Freya lay there and pondered.

She.

The woman in his arms, and that was enough for him.

He.

Freya understood now the bliss of no names.

'He's an ex.' Freya answered the question after a very long pause. 'And he tried it on last night. Several times.'

'I'd try it on again with you…'

'He's married.'

'Bastard,' Zack said. 'Did you know that he was when you were together?'

'He wasn't married then,' Freya said. 'From the way we broke up it would seem he wanted a wife and children. He's got what he wanted but his wife wasn't there last night. He said he wanted to bring in the New Year with me up in his room.'

'What did you say to him?'

'I told him I hadn't enjoyed sex with him the first time around and that I felt sorry for his short-suffering wife.'

He laughed.

'You're not married, are you?' Freya checked.

He could lie, she guessed, but she felt he wouldn't.

There was no point in lying.

'Oh, no,' Zack said. 'And I have no intention to ever be. This is absolutely guilt-free sex, baby...'

Freya doubted this encounter would be entirely guilt free, no doubt she'd be crawling with shame a few hours from now, but that was her.

'Do you have any New Year's resolutions?' he asked.

'Many,' Freya said. She had pored over them for hours and had them all written out.

'Such as?'

They were mostly the same as every other year—unlike other people, who seemed to swear to go on a diet or exercise, Freya's resolution was to not embark on a sudden diet or obsess over exercise. Not that she told him that.

Neither did she tell him about the baby she wanted and her dream of having her own little family.

Nor did she tell him that she was over men. Though perhaps not completely over them, given where she was.

So she just lay there, overthinking but oddly lulled by the soothing stroke of his hands and the nudge of his erection behind her. No, there was no need to tell him about the career she wanted to tackle but had been avoiding doing so.

'I made my list of resolutions yesterday after my run,' Freya said.

'Do you run a lot?' he asked, his fingers examining her slim, toned body.

'On alternate days,' Freya said.

'And what do you do on the other one?'

'I go for a walk,' Freya said, and the threat of tears was back but she held them in, although she did admit a truth she would never dare to another. 'And I try not to run.' She was more honest with a stranger than the people closest to her and his response was kind.

He gave a light kiss to her shoulder.

'It's okay.'

He could feel her near to tears and he got that.

Anonymity at times came with deep trust, for you were at your most bare.

'I ran,' Zack said. 'Well, I'm not a runner but I ran from all that was expected of me and I'm still running.'

She couldn't imagine him running from anything.

He was so confrontational to all of her senses she could not imagine there were things he might not be able to face.

'So what list of resolutions did you make?' he asked.

She smiled as he ran a lazy hand down her body and pulled her into him.

'Making more time for the things I like.'

'And me,' Zack said, and he started to kiss her neck.

'Try new things…' Freya said, and the arm under her moved and fingers came to her small breast and stroked it.

'I like that one too.'

He pinched her nipple and she properly understood what he'd meant about him picturing her undoing his button flies because in her mind's eye she could see those brown fingers squeezing her hard. Instead of slapping him away, she took a shaky breath as he squeezed it tight again and she felt like a bud bursting.

He took her hand and put it between her legs and then, still tweaking her breasts, his other hand met hers between her legs and *they* explored her.

'Not that one,' Freya said, and he laughed into her shoulder.

'I'm just feeling you all over,' Zack said. Working out boundaries had never been more fun. 'I want to taste you all over.'

'I don't like oral,' Freya said.

God, this was freeing, just to say it outright! To declare her needs and to state what she didn't want.

'You would.'

'No, thank you.'

He took himself in his hand and aimed the head at her fingers and moistened them as she brought herself, with a very nice lot of help from him, right to the edge.

'Not yet...' he said.

'You don't dictate my orgasm,' Freya responded in a brittle voice, trying to remember how *she* dictated her world.

'Oh, but I do.'

He went against everything she believed in the bedroom but fantastically so.

He was right at her entrance and she refused to beg, she just lay on her side, hot with anticipation. The easiest thing to do would be to not play safe but he rolled away from her and she heard the tear of foil. Freya loathed the intrusion but then he was back, lifting her hair and warming up her neck again with his mouth.

'Watch my neck,' Freya warned.

'Wear your hair down.'

'Okay.'

They both smiled at the ease of the solution.

He was making a terrible mess, she was sure, and she was doing all she could not to beg when finally he slid in and she moaned because she was swollen from last night, and it hurt quite a bit.

His large thigh came over her and he took her very slowly, painstakingly so, and she pressed back, trying to hurry him.

'What would you have done if you'd come to my room?' he asked.

'Guess,' Freya said through gritted teeth. It was obvious to her they would have had sex, only he wasn't letting her get away with that.

'Would you have knocked?'

'I don't know…' She was frantic, wanting to close her eyes and just focus on her building orgasm—not be dragged into conversation.

'I'd left the door open,' he said.

'Faster…' she begged.

'Would you have knocked?' he persisted, taking her at a slow, leisurely pace.

'No.' He gave it to her faster as a reward for her answer and then slowed when she didn't elaborate.

'I'd have come in,' Freya said as he dragged out her fantasy, as he made her reveal her thoughts.

'I might have been asleep.'

He rolled her onto her stomach and crushed her with his weight and the angle had him stroke her to the edge of bliss but he refused to push her over.

'What if I'd been asleep?' he asked.

'I'd have woken you with my mouth,' Freya said because, though she loathed the thought of it, she wanted to be the woman who could do that. 'More…' she now begged. It was like he had unbuttoned her.

'More?' Zack checked, and pulled out of her. She let out a sob of frustration.

He knelt up, pulled up her hips and Freya told him exactly where her thoughts last night had been.

'I'd have got you hard with my mouth and climbed on.'

'Dirty girl.'

'Yes,' Freya said. 'I am.'

She could hear his ragged breathing and his hand hovering over her bare cheek before he gave her a light spank.

'Yes…' Freya whimpered, and she did not recognise her own voice, or her own requests. He spanked her harder and she just about came and as her hand shot between her legs to ensure she did just that, Zack spanked her again.

'More,' Freya said.

Oh, he would have loved to carry on with the spanking, but the sound of her moans and the sight of her meant he had to be inside her.

She asked for more but he told her to be quiet, disobeying her plea to spank her again as he took her.

He seared inside her and not gently.

God, she always held back now but she was asking for more, for rougher...

He just took over and she pressed her face into the mattress.

Freya came, choking out her sobs as she pulsed around him, but he did not relent and he did not come.

There was a slight curse from him and the condom was gone, she knew, it had to be. She had never had sex without one and this was amazing.

For Zack too.

The feel of her hot and swollen was more acute and the sound of her moaning. Her hand came back and she dug her nails into his thighs. He scooped an arm under her stomach and drove in harder.

She felt like a rag doll, limp everywhere except on the inside, where she was pulled taut by him.

Freya had never completely let go in sex, she had tried to and had thought she had in those little slivers of orgasm in days gone by, but she knew now she hadn't.

Rude words were uttered and her head felt as if it had turned red as he swelled and shot into her.

Her orgasm was so sexy, a clutch of muscle that drew him in, and his warm come felt like ice seeping over her hot, swollen tightness.

And he pushed and groaned and let go deep into her until they were spent.

She listened to his long, pleasured sigh as he pulled out and then another sigh as he slipped back in to where it was warm and then out he went.

He joined her and they lay on their stomachs, facing each other, sleepy, satisfied smiles on their faces.

Freya had never had this moment where nothing else mattered than this bliss.

Soon other things would but for now nothing did.

God, she had spent most of her life trying to stay in control, only to find in some things she didn't want to.

And for Zack, who, as fleeting as his relationships were, did his best to be considerate and hold back, now looked into the eyes of someone who didn't need him to.

'Sore?' he asked, running a hand over where he had spanked her.

'I'm still high.'

They lay there and Zack said something that he usually wouldn't. 'I wish I could be your alternate day...' But that sounded way too much like making plans for Zack so he made light of what he'd just said. 'Nope, you'd be hanging up your running shoes for good.'

And Freya too kept it light. 'I don't think I could deal with you even on alternate days.' She smiled.

Freya actually meant it.

He had changed everything in her very ordered world and had awoken a side to her that
she hadn't been aware existed.

They were touching down on their real worlds,
and, on a very clear day, flight-wise, it was a sur-
prisingly bumpy landing that was to come.

Maybe paradise *was* hard to leave because, as
it turned out, they did it terribly.

The buzz of her phone as a seven a.m. alarm
went off was equalled by the chime of his and
they both groaned.

'I have to go…' Freya said.

'We need to talk.'

They really did, Zack had realised.

No names definitely didn't mean no condoms.

'Look, you don't have anything to worry about
from my end.' Zack had his doctor's voice on,
not that she knew it. 'I'm always careful and I've
just had some health checks.' He dealt with all
this in a very practical, forthright way. He was
completely in work mode now, and what Freya
couldn't know was that at work Zack was a very
different man.

'You don't have to worry about me getting

pregnant.' Freya wasn't going to go into detail about her fertility issues so she let him assume she was on the Pill, but his expression remained serious, even as they lay on their stomachs facing each other. 'I had some blood work done this week,' Freya said. 'It was all fine.' His expression was still grim and she was starting to get annoyed. 'I can go and get my computer if you don't believe me.' Her voice was rising. 'It was a torn condom, for God's sake.'

Accidents happened!

Just never to her.

Freya made sure of it.

She sat up, not liking all she had told him.

This man knew more about her than she'd told anyone and it was getting harder and harder to look him in the eye.

Zack sat up, knowing he hadn't handled that well. He tried to improve the sudden drop in atmosphere. 'Let's get some breakfast…' He'd made her feel bad and that hadn't been his intention, but in his line of work Zack had to be sure.

The snooze alarm went off and he swiped it

and then picked up the hotel phone and ordered breakfast for two.

'Coffee?' he checked.

Freya shook her head. 'I'll have a green tea.'

He ordered and then climbed from the bed. 'I'll just have a shower...' Zack said, and threw her one of the robes. 'In case breakfast arrives while I'm in there.'

He turned on the cold tap and, apart from the issue that needed to be discussed, Zack felt amazing. So much so that he was considering not just explaining that his career was the reason he needed more information but breaking their game and finding out names.

Seeing her again.

Freya.

Just as he'd predicted it would, overnight her name had come to him.

It couldn't be!

Zack turned off the shower and stepped into the bedroom, and saw that she had gone. The robe lay on the bed and her clothes and shoes were gone, and Zack let out a breath for his poor handling of things. He went into his laptop and pulled up the glossy brochure that had been sent along with the forms he'd had to fill in.

There was a photograph of the luxurious Hollywood Hills Medical Center, where he was to be interviewed this morning. He scrolled through several photographs of the doctors and nurses who practised there but Zack bypassed them and went to the section near the end.

He had already looked her up.

A few flirty emails had had him curious as to what Freya Rothsberg looked like.

Zack looked at the photo and remembered being in Nepal and checking out who the woman at the end of the emails was. It was a head shot and her long hair was blonde and straight in this image, unlike the curly brunette of last night. Here it was sleek and worn up and her make-up was neutral and she was wearing a dark grey dress with a high neck and capped sleeves.

She looked corporate and elegant and almost unrecognisable from the sultry beauty of last night.

Still, it explained better to Zack why they'd ignited on sight—for a couple of weeks up till Christmas they'd been flirting!

CHAPTER FIVE

ZACK READ THROUGH their email exchanges in the taxi on the way to The Hills.

At first it had been a semi-formal 'Dear Zackary' type of exchange.

Zack had been head-hunted by James Rothsberg and he'd had some questions about the charitable side of things so James had flicked over to Freya some of the questions that he had raised.

To: ZCarlton@ZackaryCarlton.com
From: Freya.Rothsberg@TheHollywoodHillsClinic.com
Dear Zackary,
James has passed your concerns on to me and I hope I can address them.

For some time The Hollywood Hills has been looking into a suitable charity to partner and support.

The highly regarded Bright Hope Clinic was chosen. The clinic treats underprivileged children and is situated in the south of LA, where its services are desperately needed in the densely populated area. As a result their facilities and equipment are severely stretched.

The partnership of the Bright Hope Clinic with The Hollywood Hills aims to increase the number and scope of cases that can be treated. We are lucky to have world-class facilities and can also allow for easy transfer of emergency or overseas patients using the Hills' helicopter or ambulance transport system. The Bright Hope Clinic in South LA will still run as usual, with cases requiring more complex care being referred to the Bright Hope at The Hollywood Hills.

Sincerely,

Freya Rothsberg

Public Relations Consultant

To: Freya.Rothsberg@TheHollywoodHillsClinic.com

From: ZCarlton@ZackaryCarlton.com

All good. I'll take a look into the Bright Hope Clinic and get back to you with any questions.
Zack

To: ZCarlton@ZackaryCarlton.com
From: Freya.Rothsberg@TheHollywoodHillsClinic.com
Dear Zackary,
I have attached some further information on the Bright Hope Clinic as well as the names of some contacts I have there, who would be happy to answer any of your questions.
Sincerely,
Freya Rothsberg

To: Freya.Rothsberg@TheHollywoodHillsClinic.com
From: ZCarlton@ZackaryCarlton.com
Zack!
Please can you email the forms and brochures on The Hills, the postal service is a bit slow in Nepal. Also, I note that you have the same surname as James and wondered if The Hills is a family-led clinic?

Zack loathed the politics of work and the thought of butting up against husband and wife with their own agendas held no appeal.

To: ZCarlton@ZackaryCarlton.com
From:Freya.Rothsberg@TheHollywoodHillsClinic.com
Dear Zack!
Please find attached the brochure that will better explain the clinic structure.
To address your concern—James is my brother. So, no, there aren't twenty Rothsbergs or husband-and-wife teams :-)
Freya!

He grinned that she'd read between the lines and understood his concerns.

To: Freya.Rothsberg@TheHollywoodHillsClinic.com
From: ZCarlton@ZackaryCarlton.com
Good to know!
Zack!

Flicking through the brochure, he had smiled again when he'd seen who he was dealing with and on a rather long night in Nepal he'd responded again.

To: Freya.Rothsberg@TheHollywoodHillsClinic.
com
From: ZCarlton@ZackaryCarlton.com
I meant good to know that there aren't hundreds of you, as opposed to your marital status.
Zack!

He'd regretted sending it, because Zack never flirted or got involved with anyone at work, but it had been such a subtle flirt that she probably hadn't got it.

Two days had passed and he'd actually forgotten when her response had come back.

Oh, she'd got it.

To: ZCarlton@ZackaryCarlton.com
From: Freya.Rothsberg@TheHollywoodHillsClinic.
com
Zack!
Is there a question mark missing in the previous email?
Freya!

No he never got involved with people at work, but a quickie with the PR rep surely didn't count, Zack had thought, and there were slim pickings where he'd been that night and it was nice to dream.

To: Freya.Rothsberg@TheHollywoodHillsClinic.com
From: ZCarlton@ZackaryCarlton.com
?

Her response?
There hadn't been one.
His next email, after a long day of surgery followed by a very long night in Nepal:

To: Freya.Rothsberg@TheHollywoodHillsClinic.com
From: ZCarlton@ZackaryCarlton.com
??

To: ZCarlton@ZackaryCarlton.com
From: Freya.Rothsberg@TheHollywoodHillsClinic.com
Very single. (Don't tell James.)

To: Freya.Rothsburg@TheHollywoodHillsClinic.com
From: ZCarlton@ZackaryCarlton.com
I never kiss and tell.

He smiled as he finished reading and did a quick search on her name, and suddenly Zack wasn't smiling.

There was an article on Freya, accompanied by a picture of her collapsed and being taken out of a nightclub and he read about her drug habit. There was a quote from her mother, stating that Freya was finally getting the help she needed and was in rehab.

He thought of the woman who had slunk out of his hotel room rather than face the music.

Oh, yes, they needed to talk!

Freya wasn't proud that she had dressed and left but she hadn't wanted last night to dissolve into a terse exchange.

And neither had she liked how one minute they'd been so, so intimate and the next he had reduced it to a lab-report exchange. She'd heard the shower being turned on and had gone red in the face as she'd recalled her pleas and her demands, and what had felt fine—in fact, amazing—just a short while ago had then felt like an embarrassing mistake.

She'd pulled on her dress and slipped out of his suite, taking the walk of shame back to her own room. Once in there she had surprised herself by letting out a shocked burst of laughter.

Who knew?

Not she.

Freya showered and massaged loads of conditioner into her hair and then as she dried herself off she looked at her body, turning to see her red butt cheeks. God, she felt better for it. And, now that she thought about it more calmly, Freya liked the head-on way he had tackled the awkward subject.

She'd print off her results, Freya decided. She would cross out her name and other details and put the relevant part in an envelope and leave it at Reception to be delivered to his room.

Freya got ready and dried her hair so that it was

its usual straight self, and was about to put it up
when she remembered why she couldn't.

The memory of them had her wanting more.
Freya did her best to quell a building want and
she pulled out of her wardrobe the dress she had
worn before the bridesmaid outfit.

It had been a one-off, a little sexual adventure and one that was never to be repeated again,
Freya told herself.

She pulled on a neutral linen shift that she wore
with flat ballet pumps and she carefully did her
very neutral make-up then gave a sigh of relief
when she finally recognised herself in the mirror.

Freya.

She called down to Reception and asked for
her car to be brought around and decided that,
given she had late check-out and Red was feeding Cleo, she would come back after the interview to pack. She took the elevator and went to
one of the juice bars in the foyer and ordered her
regular blend along with a nutrition bar and she
was back in control.

Freya headed over to the business centre and

printed the necessary form off, blacked out all details except the relevant part and lined up at Reception. The want and desire for him wasn't diminishing in the way she'd hoped.

It was building.

If anything, the thought of never seeing him again, of it really having been just one night had her hesitate when the receptionist asked if she could help her.

'Could I check in for another night?' Freya asked.

'Sure.' The receptionist smiled. 'I'll just check that we don't have anyone incoming for your room. No, that's fine. Is there anything else I can do for you?'

'Yes,' Freya said. 'Could I have another card for my room, please?'

'Of course.'

It took just a few seconds but Freya knew what a monumental few seconds they were. The receptionist popped the card into a little wallet with Freya's room number on it, but instead of putting it in her bag Freya put it in the envelope along with her blood results.

'Could you please deliver this to room 2812?' Freya asked, determinedly not blushing, telling herself that the receptionist would not care or even guess what she was up to.

'Sure.' The receptionist smiled. 'I'll make sure that's done for you. Is there anything else I can help you with?'

'That's it, thanks.'

Oh, my!

Freya was all flustered as she drove to work and then parked in her reserved spot at The Hills.

It really was stunning. James had put everything into the place and the patient list read like a who's who of the film industry. They did a lot more than just cosmetic procedures here, though. From obstetrics to intensive care, everything was luxuriously catered for. Well, everything except eating disorders, but Freya was planning on addressing that.

Just not today.

Today she had this interview to get through, but there was one good thing about last night, Freya thought—it had made a tiny email flirt seem pretty tame.

Yes, she'd get through the interview and then head back to the hotel and wait and see if lightning did strike twice.

Freya walked through the entrance into the foyer with its marble floor and pillars and stunning floral arrangements that were changed daily. A huge chandelier shed a calming light and Freya did her best to walk as if she hadn't been having torrid sex all night.

Sometimes the luxury of The Hills gnawed at Freya.

All her life, disparity had. She could remember tours of Africa with her famous parents. Seeing the utter poverty and then taking off in a luxury jet had felt so wrong. Being photographed with people who walked miles just for water and then watching her mother guzzling champagne for hours and bemoaning her menu selection later had made Freya furious.

Her questions to her parents had gone pretty much unanswered. 'Why are they hungry and we're not?' Freya had asked. 'I just don't get it.'

'We're doing our bit,' had been Aubrey's dis-

missive response, and her father, Michael, had had no time for his daughter's questions either.

'Freya, can you just, for five minutes, stop trying to change the world.'

James *had* listened, though, when Freya had approached him, and now things were finally getting under way.

'Hi, Freya.' Stephanie, the receptionist, smiled. 'James said to go straight through to his office.'

Freya nodded and promptly ignored Stephanie's instruction by heading for her own office. Yesterday evening James had finally sent Freya the bio for the cardiac paediatrician. He kept all staff files himself and there were no sneak peeks, even for his sister.

She wanted to read up on Zackary Carlton rather than explain to James that she was utterly unprepared for this interview. She was usually meticulous in preparation and her intention had been to read up on Zack over a leisurely breakfast this morning.

She opened up her laptop and accessed the

file but looked over as there was a knock on her open door.

'Freya,' James said. 'I asked Stephanie to tell you to come straight though.'

'Happy New Year to you too.' Freya smiled at her brother. 'Stephanie did ask me to go straight in but I'm just having a quick read through.'

'I'll deal with all the medical stuff, you just need to explain the publicity side of things and get a decent bio, so we can get the word out he's on board.' James gestured for her to come to his office and Freya picked up her laptop and went with him.

'Is he on board, though?' she asked.

'He has to be. We need this guy,' James said as they arrived at his office.

Freya took a tentative seat and thanked the spanking gods he'd stopped when he had, and she started to scroll through the file as James spoke.

'I'll bring you up to speed—Zackary Carlton. Australian, drifter, arrogant bastard. He won't commit to more than three months anywhere but, God, he does magic with his hands...'

Indeed he did.

Freya looked at the résumé and very impressive bio. There was also a photo attached and, yes, she could concur, Zackary Carlton made magic with his hands.

It was Him!

The man she had thought was safely in one of the clinic's luxurious apartments reserved for visiting guests had been staying at the hotel all along.

Freya felt sick.

And doubly so when she thought of the daiquiri-laced emails she'd sent him.

It was the same man!

How could she possibly face him?

Quite simply, Freya couldn't.

'James,' Freya croaked.

'What?'

But Freya couldn't answer straight away. After all, how did she tell her brother that she'd had random sex last night with the cardiac surgeon he wanted to hire?

'Do you really need me here for this interview?' Freya attempted. 'I've got the worst hangover. I actually feel a bit sick.'

'You hardly drink.'

'Well, I did last night,' Freya lied. 'I really think I need to go home…'

'Freya, you couldn't even begin to match my hangover,' James said, and as the intercom buzzed and interrupted him, it would seem her nightmare had just arrived.

That sexy, somewhat scruffy man she'd met yesterday scrubbed up terribly well.

He was clean shaven and wearing a dark suit in a lightweight fabric. His hair was so thick that it was still a touch damp from the shower he had been in when Freya had run, and she wanted to run again now.

Absolutely she did. So much so that Zack watched her eyes dart to the door.

Poor thing, he thought.

Zack was also surprised, not that he showed it. He hadn't expected her to be on the interview panel and seeing her face pale, rather than redden, he did what he could to put her at ease.

'James.' He shook James's hand. 'It's good to meet you.' He turned then to her. 'Freya…'

She swallowed.

'I saw you in the brochure,' he explained as he took a seat, and her embarrassment turned into anger.

He knew who she was.

Which meant that he'd known who she was last night.

Zack's teeth gritted as he saw her eyes flash in anger and he realised that, far from putting her at ease, he'd made things worse.

James and his very real hangover were going through the mountain of forms that had come in about the man he would hopefully be recruiting.

'You said no to the apartment?' James checked as he caught up on some finer details. 'Was there a problem?'

'Not at all. I just prefer to stay in hotels,' Zack said.

'What about if you work here?'

'Same,' Zack answered.

James was one of the most in-demand cosmetic surgeons in Los Angeles and he looked over at Zack, who was highly in demand too, and he chose not to play games.

'Look, I'm not going to waste your time or

mine with small talk. We want you on board. The Hills needs a cardiac surgeon specialising in paediatrics and we want it to be you.'

Zack gave an appreciative nod. He preferred people who cut to the chase.

'The only issue I have,' James continued, 'is that you're only prepared to commit to three months.'

'Then you have an issue,' Zack said, and Freya blinked at his assertion. She had never met anyone so in command of themselves.

'We're going to be building your profile and reputation and for that we'd hope—' James started.

'Now there are two issues,' Zack interrupted. 'I don't need my profile or my reputation to be built, they already speak for themselves.'

'They do,' James said. 'But our partner, the Bright Hope Clinic, desperately needs funds. I see you're keen to do some pro bono work.'

'That's the main attraction.' Zack nodded. 'Working on these cases with top-level facilities is an enticing prospect.'

'How many charitable cases were you thinking of taking on?' James asked.

'One a week during my regular list and I'll also
do a full pro bono list one Sunday a month.'

There was a lot of good that he could do in
three months, Freya thought.

'I've brought Freya in to discuss the PR side
of things.'

'I don't get involved with any of that.' Zack
shook his head and looked at her and she recognised his voice. It was the one he had used on
her that morning when they'd discussed the condom issue. He was now utterly engaged in work.
Only Freya was scorching with embarrassment,
because Zack was looking at her and talking to
her exactly as if they'd never met. 'If I come on
board I won't be doing interviews and happy smi-
ley photos. I'm sure young Paulo won't mind. I
hear no other surgeon wants to touch him.'

'Correct,' James said.

Paulo was five years old and had been brought
to the Bright Hope Clinic from Mexico with his
single mother, Maria. His complex cardiac problems meant that no surgeon would operate on

him as it was very possible that he wouldn't survive surgery.

'It happens a lot.' Zack nodded. 'I take on high-risk patients that others refuse to go near.'

'I've explained that to Freya,' James said, 'and I've spoken with my colleagues. We're all agreed that we're not involving ourselves in charity to fudge figures just to make us look good. We want to do some necessary work and that involves risks.'

'I'd only operate if I thought there was a chance,' Zack said, and James nodded. 'I focus on the surgery,' Zack continued, and turned to Freya. 'That's it.'

He was arrogant, utterly immutable, and if Freya wasn't so angry that he'd known who she was all along, she could possibly have jumped on his lap and started purring.

She didn't know how she could simultaneously be embarrassed and cross while also being impossibly turned on.

'I work on short-term contracts and the patients benefit from that.' Zack further explained his stance. 'I might not be around to do the follow-up but they have my skill and attention in the operating theatre, or the OR, or whatever the terminology is you use here. In Nepal I was working in a field hospital so I can't wait to use the amazing facilities here. I am up to date with technology and I am also very hands on with the basics…'

Freya crossed her legs.

'Will you consider extending your contract?' James asked. 'If things are going well?'

'I'll speak with you after a month.' Zack conceded the smallest fraction. 'If I can commit for another three months, I'll let you know then. If I can't commit to more than that it will give you time to start looking. I am, though, going to Australia for a couple of weeks in April.'

'To visit family?' James asked, and Freya blinked as Zack simply didn't answer the question.

Yes, they were being told that what Zack did in his own time was his concern only.

And then Freya glimpsed again the joy of anonymity and the pain of it going wrong. Zack had told her in bed this very morning that he was running from stuff. Their gazes met briefly and then Zack flicked his away and she saw his neck stretch in slight discomfort.

Oh, she wanted to know this man.

'So, when could you start?' James asked.

'I just have to sort a couple of details out and then I can let you know.'

Freya's phone buzzed and James tensed. He loathed texts and Freya rolled her eyes at his familiar response. 'It's mine.'

She glanced in her bag and saw that it was Mila.

'Sorry about that,' Freya said.

'Do you have any questions for Freya?' Jack asked.

'I do but I'll speak with her later,' Zack said.

'I...' Freya was about to say she couldn't hang around but she knew she was just putting off the inevitable. 'Sure.'

'I'll send Zack through to you when we're done.'

'Thanks,' Freya said. 'It was nice meeting you, Zack.'

Her voice was pleasant and her lips smiled, but her eyes told him what a bastard he was.

She went into her office and her skin was crawling with embarrassment and she pressed her fingers into her eyes.

This was, very possibly, going to be the longest three months of her life.

'Freya?'

She turned at the sound of Stephanie's voice.

'Are you okay?'

'Just…' Freya took a breath. 'A bit dizzy,' she explained. 'It was a big night last night.'

'Sure,' Stephanie said and handed over some files and then left.

Great, Freya thought. Stephanie just loved to have her nose in everyones business.

No doubt, that Freya was dizzy, would soon work its way back to James.

Freya made the call she had just missed.

'How are you?' Mila asked.

'You really don't want to know,' Freya said.

'Oh, but I do.' They both laughed. 'I'll have to prise it out of you later.'

She'd better not! Freya thought.

'I just wondered if there was any news about

that surgeon for Paulo? I've got Geoff, his cardiologist, here now and he's concerned.'

'He's in with James now. Let me…' Freya glanced up as James and Zack came to the door. 'I have to go,' Freya said hurriedly. 'I'll call you back.'

Zack noticed her cheeks redden and that Freya was flustered as she quickly ended the call.

'All okay?' James checked, because Freya was usually completely together, or did everything to appear to be.

She was behaving very oddly today.

'Of course it is,' Freya said. 'I thought you were giving Zack a tour.'

'We're going to do that at eleven. I've just got a patient that needs a quick review. If you can get started on the paperwork, and a head shot so that everything is in order, that would be great. We'll also need you to write up a press release and let the world know we've got Zack on board.'

'Sure.'

'Oh, and I'll ring the Bright Hope Clinic and see about getting the child looked at by Zack today,' James said.

'I can do that,' Freya offered.

'Do what?'

'Arrange his transfer.'

'Zack has to see the patient first.' James frowned. 'Since when did you start acting as a receptionist? I'll leave Zack with you.'

He walked out and Zack stood and watched as Freya picked up the phone.

'Could you give me a moment, please?' Freya asked.

'Sure,' Zack said, and stood there.

'I meant I'd like a moment of privacy, please,' she snapped, and Zack stared at her for a second before exiting her office, closing the door behind him.

God, this morning was a disaster, she thought as she frantically called Mila back.

'You haven't told James about me yet,' Mila said. 'Have you?'

'No,' Freya admitted. 'And he's just about to call the clinic.'

'It's fine,' Mila said. 'I don't generally man the phones. I'll have him put through to Geoff, but,

Freya, he needs to know that the Bright Hope Clinic is mine.'

'I know he does and I am going to tell him.'

'If you can't do it face to face, just text him.'

'He hates texts.'

'Well, he's going to hate finding out that we're going to be working together a whole lot more.'

'Leave it with me.'

Freya ended the call, took a breath and opened the door on her currently more overwhelming problem. Zack was leaning up against a wall outside and not looking very impressed to have been asked to step outside. 'Sorry about that! Come on through,' Freya said, and put on her bright corporate smile and stepped back to let him in. She waited till the door was safely closed for the smile to go and then she let him have it.

'You knew...'

'No.' He gave a small shake of his head.

'You weren't even surprised when you walked in. It was supposed to be one night, no names...'

'I thought you looked vaguely familiar but it only clicked this morning when I was in the shower,' Zack said. 'I just looked you up, and you were quite a wild child, it would seem.'

He thought of the photos of her collapsed and being carried out of a nightclub that he had seen, and he thought of the article he had read that spoke of drugs and alcohol and a lengthy stint in rehab.

'I'm not discussing this here,' Freya said. 'I don't bring my private life to work.'

'And neither do I,' Zack said. 'So go and get some blood work done and then tell me when I can start work.'

Where were the green eyes that had locked with hers last night? Oh, he was looking right at her but his expression was serious.

Grim.

'I'm a cardiac surgeon and this morning we had unprotected sex and it would appear you've had a habit. I'd like a little more than your word that you're not using.'

And she could only find a grudging admiration that he had the guts to address it directly.

'I've never done drugs.' She looked at him. 'I

did have some tests last week and they all came back clear.'

'Has there been anyone since then?'

'Zack!'

'Freya, don't play coy. You've got all my lab results sitting on your desk, I haven't been with anyone since I had blood pulled, and I sure as hell haven't been in rehab. So I need to know the score.'

'I had some blood work for fertility issues and they ran the tests as routine. I was in rehab for an eating disorder. Happy now?'

'Well, *happy* isn't the word I'd use to find out the condom split with someone having fertility treatment, but, yep, glad to know we're both clean.'

'Well, you don't have to worry about the fertility issue. I haven't started treatment and I shot my ovaries.'

'Shot your ovaries?' Zack frowned and then got it.

Her eating disorder meant she couldn't have kids and he understood better now what she'd told him about running and trying not to.

'I'll let James know that I can start straight away, then.'

He gave her a nod and turned to go but Freya halted him. 'Zack, you won't—'

'Freya.' He turned around. 'I'd never say anything and, as you're about to find out, I'm a very different person at work.'

'Sure.'

'The only reason I am talking about last night in this office is because it's pertinent to work. What happened is not to be brought up or discussed, do you understand that?'

'Yes.'

It was the longest day.

All she wanted to do was go home and curl up with her shame, yet, now that Zack was on board, her life had gotten busy.

His résumé was impressive on a professional level. He'd worked all over the globe, in both lavish and sparsely equipped hospitals. She looked up his hometown and her eyes widened when she read about the tiny population and how widely it was scattered.

Well, they could go with the country-boy angle, Freya thought, and then tried to picture herself suggesting that to Zack.

Ah…perhaps not.

What else could she find out?

It would seem that five years ago he'd been in Canada at an ice hockey match when a player had gone into cardiac arrest and Zack had successfully resuscitated him.

A couple of phone calls later and she was in touch with the player's own PA. Nothing was said, just a little touching base query to see if the player might be open to being flown to LA.

'He's on vacation but I'll get back to you at an *appropriate* time.'

God, no wonder people were tense, Freya thought as she realised that most of the world considered today not really a day for such calls, but at The Hills, though there were no scheduled operations, it was a work day as usual.

The staff up on the cardiac unit didn't say, *Oh, no, it's a holiday,* as they prepared the bed for Paulo to arrive.

And neither did the pilot of the luxury helicopter question it when, after examining Paulo and going through his tests at the Bright Hope Clinic, Zack called James.

'I've just spoken with Maria, his mother,' Zack said. 'I've told her that I'm still not sure if he's a candidate for surgery but I would like to run some more tests at The Hills. Their equipment is terrible.'

And so by three that afternoon a new little patient with black hair and eyes and a gappy smile was sitting in bed with his worried mother by his side.

And by five all Freya wanted was home and was struggling to hold it together when James knocked at her door.

'He's not very sociable, is he?' James rolled his eyes. 'I tried to schedule a meeting and he wants it to be held in a meeting room, rather than my office. Neutral territory, he said.'

Freya actually laughed.

'Three months in a hotel…' James shook his head. 'The guy's a well-dressed gypsy. I've asked him to come and get a security tag—can you please sort out his head shot?'

'I shall,' Freya said.
She'd sort it tomorrow.
All she wanted now was home.

CHAPTER SIX

So DISTRACTED WAS Freya that she forgot she'd booked in for another night at the hotel until she was nearly home. Freya decided to check in on Cleo and then head back, grab her stuff and just come home and sleep away the shame.

She really wanted to curl up and pull the covers over her head and hibernate till the end of March when Zack would be gone but knew that wasn't going to happen.

Freya parked and went up to her apartment, and as she opened the door she saw that her neighbour Red was just on his way out after feeding her little pug, Cleo.

'Hi.' Freya smiled.

'How are you, Freya?'

'I'm well! Thanks so much for this.'

'No problem. Are you back for the night?'

'I'm not sure,' Freya said, deciding she might just crash at the hotel. 'If I'm not here, can you let her out for me?'

'Of course.'

She had great neighbours and favours were freely given and returned. Red told her that he'd watched a movie last night with Cleo and had had a couple of beers.

Freya thanked him again and kept her smile on and wide, and only when Red had gone did she sink down onto the sofa and let her smile fade. She rested her head in her hands and just sat with the panic that had been chasing her all day since she'd worked out who Zack was.

'Oh, Cleo...'

She picked up her little, fat friend and told her all of it, well, not in specific detail, but that she'd lost her head last night to the most gorgeous of men on the promise they would never again meet.

'And now I have to work alongside him for three months. I don't know what to do.'

Cleo gave her no answers, just snuffled. The little pug was the absolute love of her life. James had bought her for Freya on her discharge from rehab and Freya had finally found a soul she could pour her heart out to.

'How can I face him?' she asked her fur baby.

Freya cuddled her for a good hour and then she carried her down for her little walk. Cleo was getting so tired and so old and Freya knew she wouldn't have her for much longer. James, because he was concerned how Freya would cope when her beloved companion died, had suggested, under the guise that it might give Cleo a new lease of life, that Freya get a puppy.

'I don't want another dog,' Freya said to Cleo as she popped her onto the sofa.

And not just because she could never love another dog as much as this one.

Freya wanted a baby. She was so over attempts at relationships and had no qualms about being a single mom.

She couldn't do a worse job than her parents had, and they'd been together till Freya was thirteen.

As she drove back to the hotel, Freya felt drained and exhausted. She'd had basically no sleep all night and the most awkward, uncomfortable of days and, joy, she had to face him again tomorrow.

She stood in the elevator and tried not to think of what had taken place such a short while ago and then she wearily swiped open her hotel door.

And there, just sitting there, drink poured, tie loose and wearing a triumphant grin, waving an envelope, was Zack. He just watched Freya groan as she remembered the room card she'd left.

'One night, no names?' Zack checked, holding up the envelope.

And when you've been truly caught, all you can really do is admit it.

'Two nights, then,' Freya said. 'I never said I didn't enjoy it.'

'Great, wasn't it?' Zack grinned. 'Well, thank you for the test results. That was actually very good of you. So good of you that I'm here to service you. Get over here.' He stamped the floor with his boot.

'I thought we were never to discuss it again.'

'At work it is never to be brought up,' Zack said. 'Out of work is a completely separate thing. So come here.'

Oh, now she understood better his stance on not answering questions.

'I can't,' Freya said. 'I'm so embarrassed.'

'Don't be.' He grinned. 'Come here.'

Freya made her way over and he pulled her onto his lap and she was just one burning blush but he was laughing.

'I really don't get involved with people I work with,' Freya said. 'Dating and—'

'Guess what,' Zack interrupted. 'I don't date.'

'Never?'

'Nope,' Zack said. 'So don't worry about awkward stuff and holding hands and all that sort of thing. Poor us, just sex.'

'Oh, no.'

'Liar, liar…' And her knickers *were* on fire because he slipped a hand up her dress.

'And you don't have to worry, no one will ever hear your secret from me.'

'Secret?' Freya frowned.

'That the uptight Freya likes a bit of no-name spanky on the down-low.'

'Zack,' she said, 'I didn't know till last night

that I liked that…' She looked at him and could tell he didn't believe her. 'I'm not like that.'

'Freya, you emailed me a couple of weeks ago and said you were *very* single and not to tell James.'

'That was after a very difficult night being told by my soon-to-be-married and married friends that it would be my turn next. I'd had too much to drink and decided to live a little. Believe it or not, you're the only person I'd been with for the whole of last year.'

'Well, given we saw in the New Year downstairs, you had no one last year, Freya, so you have some catching up to do.'

'I don't think so,' Freya said, yet she was fighting not to undo the buttons on his shirt.

'I'm here for three months,' Zack said, 'and we're both as clean as whistles. Though, given we couldn't get through one night without tearing the rubber, you need to get on the Pill. I really don't want to rely on your shot ovaries, as you so fondly refer to them.'

'Zack, we can't.'

'But you know that we shall.'

Freya said nothing, he was so assured they'd be back in bed.

Sadly for her self-control, he was completely right—she was already unzipping him and taking it out.

'Don't tell James...'

CHAPTER SEVEN

ZACK REALLY WAS a master at keeping his private life separate from work.

By day he was remote, perhaps even a bit unfriendly at times. There were absolutely no shared looks, or exchanges, not even behind closed doors.

He dived straight into a very full schedule but occasionally Freya found herself back at the hotel, and, yes, the sex was amazing but they didn't talk much. She knew some stuff, but the information he shared was as generous as a waiter with the cracked pepper—there was never enough.

They lay there one morning and he was the monkey on her back, unknotting all her muscles, when he asked her something.

'Why are you avoiding James?'

'I'm not,' Freya said, and he felt her shoulders stiffen.

'Who were you speaking to on the phone the morning of my interview?'

'I can't remember.'

'You got all flustered.'

'Well, my one and only one-night stand suddenly had a name.'

'Tell me,' he said, 'were you on the phone to some guy?'

'A woman, actually,' Freya said, and he laughed.

'Do tell.'

'Nope.' The fewer people who knew about Mila and James's rocky past the better. And the fewer who knew about her and Zack's torrid present, all the better too!

'How come you stay here?' Freya asked as breakfast was served. Coffee for him, green tea and avocado smash for Freya.

'I just like it.'

'But you could have an apartment.'

'I don't want one.'

'Well, if you've got money to burn...'

'I've been sleeping under a mosquito net for six months,' Zack pointed out.

'Even so...'

Freya stayed quiet.

It wasn't money that was the issue, it was his transient existence that irked her.

Everything he had was in this room and he could check out tomorrow, Freya knew. His time in one place was only as long as his theatre list.

'Are you going to operate on Paulo?'

He didn't answer at first then he said, 'Is that PR Freya or Freya asking?'

'Freya.'

'Yes, I'm just trying to get him at optimum health first. You know his mother lost another son?'

Freya nodded.

'I don't want her losing two.'

And he watched as she cracked a very generous amount of cracked pepper on her avocado.

'My brother died nearly ten years ago. I saw what losing one kid did to my mother.'

For Freya, to hear Zack suddenly reveal such a

vital part of himself, it was like the cracker had fallen off the pepper mill.

'Zack! I'm so sorry to hear that.'

He grinned. 'Don't use your psychologist voice on me.' Then he asked her something he was curious about. She'd told him about her psychology degree and he wanted to know why she didn't use it. 'I know you're good at PR but do you really enjoy it?'

'I do,' Freya said, and she took a breath and told him her plans, wondering if he'd laugh. 'I want to start seeing clients. I wasn't ready to before.'

'Ready?'

'I just didn't know if I had any right to advise on eating disorders when I was working so hard on myself. I'm not sure I'm ready even now.'

'I'd say you're ready.' Zack smiled. 'I've spoken more to you than I have to anyone. You're very easy to talk to, Freya.'

'You're not.' She smiled back, glowing on the inside that he thought she could do it, but then she was serious. She really wanted to know more about him. 'How did your brother die?' she asked.

'How we all die,' Zack said, refusing to open

up on her demand. He told only what he wanted to. 'His heart stopped beating.'

Aaagh! He was so frustrating but when he shared a part of himself it just made her want to know more.

'Head injury.' Zack relented a touch.

'Do you miss him?'

'I do,' Zack said, and he liked it that she didn't say that he must miss him. 'It's always there in the background, other times…' He shrugged, reluctant to explain it. 'My parents, though, still grieve every day.'

'That must be hard to watch.'

'Which is why I don't,' Zack said.

Subject closed.

And so she knew something but so little about him and that was proven on his second week at work as the day of Paulo's surgery neared and Freya wanted more for another press release.

'Everything you need is on my résumé,' Zack said, clearly less than impressed to be in her office.

'Well, can we go with the small-town angle?'

'It's hardly small,' Zack snapped. 'It's the size of LA.'

'I meant the population.'

'If you bring my family into this,' Zack said, 'then you'd better find a stand-in for Paulo's surgery. Oh, that's right, you won't be able to, so you can go and tell his mother why the clinic lost the only doctor prepared to operate on her son.'

'I'll take that as no!' Freya was used to difficult doctors. Putting the new brochure together had been difficult enough, but running promo on Zack took the cake. 'Can we just get a photo of you with him?'

'I don't work like that, Freya. You're not getting your cheesy photo.'

'Fine,' Freya snapped. 'What am I supposed to write?'

'That a child from the Bright Hope Clinic with a complex tetralogy of Fallot is being operated on at The Hollywood Hills Clinic and that—'

'I've already got that part, thanks.' Tough Freya wasn't working so she lodged an appeal with her eyes but he stared back coolly and dismissed her flirt. 'People like to see the human angle.'

'Then get it elsewhere,' Zack said. 'Because it's not coming from me.'

'I still need your head shot.'

'Take it, then.'

'Do you want to go and freshen up?'

'No.'

'You haven't shaved.'

'I don't shave on the week of a big operation.'

'Really?' Freya's eyes lit up. 'Zack, that's just the type of information people want to—'

'Freya,' Zack warned, 'I'm getting tired of this.'

She took out her camera. Usually she'd dab a bit of powder on the subject's face but she didn't think it would be appreciated in this case. Usually when someone was about to have their picture taken they would now be at the mirror, fixing their hair or rearranging their tie or stethoscope.

Zack just sat there and stared back.

'Can you at least smile?'

He gave her such a fake smile that Freya actually laughed. 'I'll settle for scowling.'

She got her shot and it was actually an incredibly good one.

'Can I go now?'

'Sure. Do you want to come over tonight?' she asked, but he just stood up and walked off.

Zack kept her hanging.

Oh, they'd agreed to never discuss the other side of them at work, but just some indication about where she stood might be nice.

Except she knew where she stood.

Zack had made it very clear.

He didn't come to her apartment. They played at his hotel.

Which meant she should not be sending her phone a copy of his photo and she should not be wondering, hoping, that night as she left work, if Zack was going to call.

He did.

Or rather he fired a text that night at eight to see if she wanted to meet at the bar of the hotel.

She wanted him to come to her home.

Freya fired back her answer.

Busy tonight.

She wasn't.

Well, there was always work she could catch up on but she was starting to struggle with her end of things.

No problem.

Zack's response annoyed her.

There were no questions or comment, no *I miss you*, no *Pity*. There was nothing to indicate that her response mattered to him.

It did.

Zack was actually relieved that Freya said no to coming to the hotel.

Well, not relieved in a sexual sense, just that he knew now that he would not be seeing her again socially for several days now.

They were getting too involved for his comfort. Too many times through the day he went to call her or saved something in his head to tell Freya about that night. Certainly he wasn't comfortable with the idea of going over to her home.

He didn't want a relationship.

He thought of his brother, chained till the day

he'd died to a life that he hadn't wanted, and it would never happen to Zack. And yet he didn't feel chained when he was with Freya, he felt more open and honest than he ever had.

It was too much to think of now.

So, yes, he was relieved that she'd declined coming over as it meant that he didn't have to worry about his increasing feelings towards Freya for now. He would be in bed early tomorrow, preparing himself for a very long operation, and he would be living more or less between his office and Paulo's bedside for a couple of days afterwards.

If Paulo made it.

CHAPTER EIGHT

ZACK WASN'T AT work the next morning.

Freya noticed.

All night she had been fighting with herself not to change her mind and go over to his hotel but really, Freya knew, she wanted more than she was getting from Zack.

'How's it all going?' James asked as Freya dropped by.

'Very well,' Freya said. 'James, I'm just going to Bright Hope to take some posters over for them to put up.'

'Well, I don't want any posters put up here,' James said.

'I wouldn't tarnish your walls,' Freya said.

'Is everything okay?' James checked.

'Everything's fine. Why?'

'You just seem…' James shrugged.

'I'm just busy and I'm also…' Freya knew that she had to tell him. Mila's name was on the posters she was holding in her arms. If the operation was a success it was going to be all over the press and it was time that her brother found out what had been going on behind his back. 'James, we need to talk.'

'Sit down, then.'

James had always made time for her and she could see the concern in his eyes. She wished he'd stop being so protective, so ready to assume that at any moment she might slip back into ways of old.

Freya was tired of being treated like glass and didn't get why they couldn't speak openly about things.

That time in their lives hurt too much, Freya guessed.

And what she was going to say now would hurt James, she guessed too, which was why she had been avoiding it.

'You know the Bright Hope Clinic…'

'What now?' James sighed. 'Freya, my charitable cup does not runneth over. I do have patients of my own.'

'I know that. It's not about a patient, it's about the founder.' She swallowed. 'Mila Brightman...'

She watched as her brother's face paled but he said nothing at first, just sat there, but then he spoke. 'Mila wouldn't get involved in anything that has my name on it.' James shook his head. 'No way.'

'Of course she would for the sake of her patients.'

'How long have you known that she's involved in Bright Hope?'

'I've always known,' Freya said. 'We've stayed friends.'

'You stayed friends with my ex?'

'She was my friend too,' Freya said.

'And you didn't think to tell me any of this?'

'It was very easy not to, you avoid the charity stuff...'

'And Mila's the reason why I do!'

'I know that.'

'No, you don't,' James snapped. 'I thought she

was overseas and all this time you two have been colluding—'

'We've been doing what we can for the patients. Come on, James, look at the amazing stuff that's happened already. Paulo's getting a chance, you've got a burns patient next—'

'Get out,' James interrupted.

'James—'

'I mean it, Freya.'

And she looked at her brother who had always been there for her, now telling her to get out.

'James,' Freya said in her most patient voice, 'let's talk about this.'

'Are you still here?' he asked. 'I'm telling you, Freya, get the hell out.'

Freya walked out his office and straight to her car. She had known that he wouldn't be pleased, but to be told to get out had been unexpected.

James couldn't choose who she was friends with.

Mila and he had been engaged, had been about to be married. Just because he had chosen not to go through with it, it didn't have to mean that she'd turn her back on Mila.

Freya was so upset that for once she didn't notice Zack walking towards her.

'Hey,' Zack said. 'Where are you off to?

'I'm just taking some posters to the Bright Hope Clinic. I'm hoping—'

'Enough.' Zack put up his hand. 'I shouldn't have asked. I'm trying not to think about tomorrow just yet.'

'Sorry,' Freya said, and she thought of the pressure he must be under.

'About last night—'

'Not here, Freya.'

'It's a car park.' Freya pointed out. 'Look, how about tonight? I could cook something. Come over—'

'Freya, not here,' Zack said again. 'We agreed.'

'Sure.' Freya said, and walked off. She loaded all the posters into her car but before she drove off she texted Zack her address and again asked if he wanted dinner. Yes, she knew she was pushing to move things along to more than they had agreed to.

She wanted things to move along, though, Freya thought.

She hit 'send' and then headed south for the Bright Hope Clinic.

'Hi,' Mila said when she arrived, and then saw Freya's tense features. 'You told James.'

Freya nodded. 'I did.' Though it wasn't just James and their row that she was feeling so tense about. She was still waiting for Zack to respond. 'It didn't go down too well.'

'How is he?'

'Shell-shocked,' Freya said. 'I think he thought you were still overseas. He pretty much left all the research of charities to me.'

Mila was busy working and Freya put up all the posters and then left. As she stepped through the door of her apartment she had her answer to dinner and her invitation to come over in a less than effusive text.

No thanks. Zack

He hadn't even put the little exclamation mark that they jokingly used in their exchanges. Oh, Freya knew it was a tiny detail but she could feel that they were slipping away from each other and she didn't want them to.

I could come over to you.

Freya read what she'd just typed and she loathed herself for it. She looked at Cleo, who just stared back at her and told her to please not do it.

She hit 'send'.

'Sorry,' she said to Cleo.

And, rather more rapidly this time than last, she got her response.

Not tonight.
I've got a big day tomorrow.
Zack

And it was there, in that second, Freya knew, that things had changed.

Maybe not for Zack.

But for her.

It wasn't just sex for her.

Maybe it never had been.

For Freya, it felt a whole lot more than anything she had ever known.

CHAPTER NINE

THINGS HAD, IN FACT, changed for Zack.

He'd declined her invitation for dinner, when he actually wanted a quiet night in with Freya, but it moved them into uncharted territory and Zack did not have the head space to explore that now.

Instead, he hit 'send' and then walked into his office to speak with Maria, which was a very difficult conversation to have.

'You've told me all this,' Maria said. 'Many times. I understand that he might not make it...'

'Maria,' Zack said, 'listen to me. You have to hear this.' They went through it again, not just the risks of the procedure but how they would deal with Paulo tomorrow as he went under anaesthetic.

He left her crying with Sonia, a skilled PICU

nurse, who would help Maria compose herself before she went back in to be with her son.

Then he got Freya's invitation to come over and sex really was the last thing on his mind and, annoyed at her persistence, he hit 'send' on a thanks, but, no, thanks text and then felt like a bastard.

She was too much, too intense, yet he liked it. Freya was complex and changeable, fragile yet strong, and he simply could not think about her now.

He lay in his hotel room, turning up the news to drown out the sound of a couple at it in the next room.

Zack couldn't face the noise and chatter of the restaurant. Instead, he ordered room service, looked at the steak he'd ordered and washed it down with a side of pasta and a couple of bottles of sparkling water. Then it was time to start thinking about tomorrow.

He knew that there was a lot riding on this operation being a success. The Bright Hope

Clinic desperately needed the donations that would start to roll in if it went well.

But it wasn't that that truly daunted him. What did, was a five-year-old with a seriously messed-up heart. That was all there was space for in his head.

Zack checked in on his ego to make sure he wasn't being cavalier, and then he phoned Cale, a mentor and friend in Australia that he'd trained under, and went through his proposed procedure with him when Zack still couldn't wind down.

Then he slept a dreamless sleep, which he had trained himself to do on the night prior to a big operation, and instead of the car he'd hired he had a taxi drive him in.

He went through things with the anaesthetist and the OR team and checked in on PICU. Paulo had been admitted there last night so he would be used to it when he came around and also to have some medications administered overnight.

'Hello, you.' He smiled at his little friend.

'Zack!'

He was groggy from light sedation but Paulo

smiled at his big friend. Zack looked over at Maria and could see she was about to crumble. 'Not now,' Zack warned, and Maria nodded, remembering the long talk they'd had yesterday.

'I'll see you in pre-op,' he said to Paulo, ruffled his hair and walked off.

He made his last checks and then he was told that Paulo and his mother were there and Zack went through.

'Did you just get more handsome?' Zack asked, and Paulo grinned his gappy blue-lipped grin.

'He's my handsome man,' Maria said. 'I love you, baby,' she said to her son. *'Te amo...'*

'Te amo, Mamma,' Paulo said.

Maria gave him a kiss and Zack watched as she cuddled him tight while the anaesthetist started to give the medicines and then, as Maria had tried so hard not to do, once he was safely under she broke down.

'Well done,' Zack said, and he gave her a hug. 'I will do all I can, Maria. You were wonderful with him.'

That was the hard part over with, thought Zack as he headed off to scrub.

Now came the harder part, eight hours of surgery.

He just hoped that today he didn't get to the hardest part—telling Maria that her beautiful son was dead.

The whole clinic was on tenterhooks throughout a very long day.

The estimated operating time of eight hours became nine.

Nine became ten and as it did so Freya's phone went again. She knew, even without looking, that it would be Mila.

She was right.

'I know you said you'd call with any updates but I'm going crazy here.'

'I've heard nothing,' Freya said. 'I'll be the very last to know if Zack has his way. He doesn't consider PR a high priority.'

'I know,' Mila said.

'It's been more than ten hours now. Is that good?' Freya asked.

'I hope so,' Mila sighed, and they chatted for ten as they hung out, waiting for news on Paulo. 'How are you and James doing now?'

'We're still not talking,' Freya admitted. 'He's been in, observing the operation.' Then she heard familiar footsteps and knew it was James heading for his office and Freya put the phone down on her desk and ran out.

'James?'

'I was just coming in to tell you. Paulo's in Recovery and Zack is, basically, amazing,' James said, and the animosity between him and Freya was temporarily cast aside for a moment just to breathe in the relief. 'It's still very early days, of course. I can see why no one wanted to touch that heart.' James shook his head. 'It was a mess, yet it was like watching a miracle to see him operate. Zack must have nerves of steel.'

And then he seemed to remember that they weren't talking and James gave her a nod and Freya went back to the phone.

'James said—'

'I heard,' Mila interrupted, and Freya sat silent as Mila started to cry. She truly didn't know if Mila was crying with relief over Paulo or hearing James's voice, or both.

God, James! Freya thought.

Why did you have to do what you did?

He had caused so much pain and though she loved her brother very much, it didn't take away her anger for all the hurt that he had caused to her friend. And the worst part of all was that Freya simply didn't know why James had decided to end things with Mila on their wedding day.

Freya sat there listening as her friend tried to pull things together.

'I have to go,' Mila said. 'Sorry to cry.'

'It's an emotional time.'

'Well, you've had plenty of them and yet you never cry,' Mila snapped. She knew how closed off Freya was and she could sense something was wrong. 'Freya, is everything okay? Apart from James and things.'

'Everything's...' Freya didn't even know where to start. Zack had made it very clear that the two of them were not to be discussed and she guessed there would be plenty of time for introspection once he had gone. 'I'll bring you up to speed soon enough.'

'I'm going to keep you to that,' Mila said. 'Can you keep me up to date with any news about Paulo?'

'Of course I shall.'

'What time are you going home?'

'I don't know,' Freya admitted.

It was the oddest night.

As the clock hit ten, Abi Thompson, a reconstructive surgeon who had viewed some of the operation from the gallery, stopped by for a chat.

'Zack was awesome,' Abi said. 'There was no music, no chatter. Zack just stopped for water and half a banana a couple of times. It was so intense in there, there were a couple of near misses—not that you'd have known from watching Zack.'

Oh, Zack knew *all* about the misses.

He stood at the end of Paulo's bed and checked all the charts with Sonia, the PICU nurse. He knew exactly how close Paulo had come to death and the surgery would certainly have turned that way if he hadn't had such state-of-the-art equipment.

Maybe he should put himself out there a bit more, if it meant more funds.

'He's going to be a doctor when he grows up,' Maria said, holding her son's hand. 'You wait, he's going to make you proud.'

Zack nodded. Maria didn't need to know that those were the words he dreaded, and why he didn't have pictures of smiling children lining a regular office.

He didn't want the strain on a teenager's face as their father shook Zack's hand and said a similar thing.

Paulo owed him nothing.

Not even a good life.

It was up to Paulo.

His life was his to live.

'Shouldn't you get something to eat?' Sonia broke into his thoughts. 'I could be calling on you a lot throughout the night.'

Zack nodded. 'I just rang down and asked for a meal to be left in my office.' Sonia was right, he had done all he could, and for now Paulo was critical but stable and there was a whole team starting to take over his care. 'I'm going to try and grab an hour of sleep,' he said. 'Page me for anything. Don't wait.'

'Sure.'

He headed down and just nodded to James, who was speaking with Stephanie at Reception. Zack was thankful that James understood he wasn't in the mood to speak and just gave him an appreciative nod back.

He walked past Freya's open door and she saw that but then Zack turned around.

'I'm not ignoring you,' he said. 'I just can't talk to anyone right now.'

'Fair enough.' Freya smiled. She was prickly about last night but wasn't selfish enough to address that now.

'I've spoken with Maria and she says you can release the news that he's out of Theatre.'

'Thanks.'

Still he didn't leave.

'Sorry about last night,' Zack said. 'I wouldn't have been much company.'

'That's fine.' And they looked at each other for

a long time, Freya trying to bite back from saying that it didn't all have to be about sex, but well aware he didn't need her stuff now.

'For what it's worth,' Zack said, 'I regretted it.'

And Freya said nothing. She guessed more than ten hours of surgery counted for a little lapse and that he might also later regret saying what he just had.

'I'm going to get something to eat.'

'Well, whatever you ordered was just delivered to your office and, I have to say, it smells amazing. Go and have a rest,' Freya said. She had never seen someone look so wiped out.

'I'm just going to try and grab an hour and then head back up there.'

'Do you want me to come and wake you?'

'Would you?'

'Sure.'

Zack went to go and then again changed his mind. 'Freya, could you take my pager and answer it? If it's PICU come and get me straight away but if it's anyone else...'

'Sure.'

'Were you going home?' Zack checked.

'Nope.'

The food was amazing, and he ate it and then rehydrated with more water. Then he lay back on the plush couch and tried not to go over the surgery in his head. He just wanted to clear his mind.

Only he couldn't.

Twice during the surgery he'd thought he'd been wrong to take the procedure on. One hour in, he had considered closing but had pushed on. Five hours in he had been certain that the heart was too much of a mess, but it wasn't as if he'd had any choice by then but to carry on.

Watching that heart start beating when it had come off bypass, he'd heard the elation in the theatre but had said nothing.

Going in to speak to Maria, he had warned her that the next forty-eight hours were critical and had been guarded with his optimism. No matter how Zack had warned her that Paulo might not make it through surgery, that the little boy had survived was more of a miracle than Maria would ever know.

Since the operation started he had not been able to relax for a moment yet now he had to.

And Freya knew that too.

His pager buzzed and when she saw that it wasn't from PICU Freya rang the switchboard. 'He's not taking any calls unless it's PICU. If you can take a message I'll pass it on.'

'Sure,' the operator said, and Freya waited and then frowned when the operator came back on. 'It's his father calling from Australia, he says that it's urgent.'

'Okay,' Freya said. What choice did she have? 'I'll let him know.'

Freya knocked on the door to his office and went in. 'Zack,' Freya said. 'Zack!'

'Is it PICU?' He sat straight up on the second call.

'No...'

'Later, Freya.'

'It's your father,' Freya said. 'He says that it's urgent.' She handed his impatient hand the phone.

'What's going on?' Zack asked. 'Is it Mum?'

He saw Freya standing there and he glanced up, about to tell her, as she had once told him, that he'd like some privacy, given it was clearly a personal call. Then he saw the concern in her face and it wasn't intrusive.

Freya saw his glance and realised she was hovering, and tried to remember the rules, but as she went to go he caught her wrist and frowned as his father spoke on. 'Zack, I need some medical advice. Do you remember Tara?'

'Of course I remember Tara, Dad.' Zack's jaw gritted—did they think he had no soul just because he hadn't stayed? 'Is she okay?'

'Tara's doing well, it's the baby that's causing me some concern.'

'Tell me.'

'He was four weeks premature and breech but healthy, they kept him in for five days and he was discharged at birth weight.

'He's fourteen days old now and for the last couple of days Tara's been coming in. The baby seems to be doing well but...'

'Dad?' Zack frowned because his father sounded hesitant yet he was the best diagnostician Zack knew.

'He's eating, he's drinking and he's crying. I

can't put my finger on it, Zack, but there's something not right. There's a big emergency north of here, only high-priority transfers…'

'What does Tara think?'

'Well, Jed—'

'Not her husband,' Zack said. 'What does Tara say?'

'She's distraught. She says that his cry has changed. I can't pick up a murmur…'

'Do you think that it's cardiac related?'

'I'm sure that it is,' his father said. 'That's why I'm calling you.'

Zack went through everything. There was some sweating but the temperatures were sky-high back home, and there was also a slight reduction in peripheral perfusion, his father felt, though that was more on instinct.

'I should get him seen but on all the guidelines he's non-urgent at this stage.'

'Dad, if he's got a ductal dependent lesion…' Zack didn't need to spell it out that these babies were all too often diagnosed at post-mortem. 'If you're worried then he needs to be seen straight away.'

'There's been a train crash and the air ambu-lances have to prioritise.'

'I don't think you called me for a chat,' Zack said.

'No.'

'He needs to be seen by Cale. I'll call him now and he'll put the baby's transfer as a priority.'

'There's not much to go on.'

'Yes, there is,' Zack said. 'You have forty years' experience, I'd take that any time. What's the baby's name?'

'Max,' his father answered. 'Zack, what if I'm wrong?'

'Then I'll be more than happy to wear it. I'll call you back when I've spoken with Cale. You tell them to send the air ambulance as a priority.'

Zack no longer felt tired now.

Freya sat on the couch as he rang his mentor and then called his father back.

'It's all sorted in Brisbane—they're expecting him. Cale's coming in and will be there when the baby arrives.'

'Thanks, Zack. We've got clearance for the air ambulance.'

Zack breathed out as he ended the call.

His head couldn't take it. The very thought of Tara going through what Maria had today brought it all too close to a personal level, which Zack did his best to avoid.

'That was my father...'

'I heard,' Freya said.

'Tara's my ex.' He shook his head. 'Too much?'

'No, I think it's nice that you care.' Freya really did, as the impression given by Zack was that he always walked away without a second glance.

'Well, my parents don't think that I do. They've both asked if I remember her, as if I've cut off the first eighteen years of my life. In fairness they never knew we were on together, but as if I'd forget a friend!' He was not going to spill it all out just because he was tired, and anyway PICU rang at that moment to alter some drug doses for Paulo.

'He's doing all the right things,' Zack said, leaning back. 'I'll go and review him at midnight, unless there's any change before then.' He glanced at his phone and Freya saw that he was looking at the time in Australia.

'What does your father think is wrong with the baby's heart?' Freya asked.

'Some defects aren't picked up at birth but when the ducts close at around a couple of weeks old… It might be nothing, it might be a small lesion that could have waited, but if my father's ringing me that means he's seriously worried because nothing would get that proud old bugger to call me otherwise.'

'Hell, I still can't believe that he did.'

'Well, you are a cardiac surgeon.'

'Ah, but he'd prefer…'

Zack stopped and then handed her the phone. 'If PICU calls…'

'Sure.'

'Or are you going home?'

'I'm staying tonight.'

'You don't usually.'

'No.' Freya didn't know what to say—she was here because she wanted to be and Zack didn't know what to say because it was actually a help to him that she was.

He didn't like leaving his pagers with others, though he had to at times, of course.

He looked at Freya and he told her more about Paulo's operation. 'I thought twice I'd lost him,' he said, and for the first time he *told* another person what he usually put in his reports, though he gave Freya a far less comprehensive version.

'And if you put any of this in your press releases...'

'I never would,' Freya said. 'I'll email them to you first if you prefer.'

Zack nodded. It felt odd to be unloading thoughts that he usually kept in his head and he was grateful that Freya, when he was too tired to do so, drew a very firm line to ensure that nothing he said he could live to regret.

'I called a colleague last night to go through the surgery I planned and also to check that it wasn't my ego taking him to Theatre. He agreed that Paulo had a chance and that he'd proceed. It's actually the guy Tara's baby has gone to. I spent a year working on his team.'

'So the baby's in good hands.' Freya smiled.

'The best of hands,' Zack said, and then continued to talk about the surgery he'd performed. 'When I first opened him up I was just going to close him and then five hours in I actually wished that I had. I was just going through the motions for the last hours, repairing what I could, remembering all I'd been taught. When they took him off bypass and I saw that heart fill…' The adrenaline that had kept him going through surgery and again when his father had called was still surging through his veins.

'I can't switch off,' Zack admitted.

'When are your days off?' Freya asked.

'I'm not going to get out of this place for the next couple of days.'

'Do you want to come riding at the weekend?' It just popped into her head and then she realised that it might be open to misinterpretation. 'I meant horses.'

He grinned. 'I got that. Do you ride?'

'Not very well,' Freya said, 'but I love it when I do, it helps me to unwind… It was a part of my rehab.'

'Really?'

Zack was about to say no but then thought about it and, yep, a few hours on horseback to look forward to sounded like a good way of staying sane during these coming days.

Freya could see, though, that he was hesitant.

'No strings, Zack. I'm not asking you out on a date.'

She'd got his back-off message yesterday loud and clear.

'I know,' Zack said. 'Are we awkward?'

'A bit.' Freya shrugged slightly. 'But that's because I've never done this before.'

'Done what?'

'Not now,' Freya said, and shook her head. Now really wasn't the time to explain how she was struggling with her feelings for him and the inevitable ending of them. Maybe there would never be a suitable time to tell him all he was starting to mean to her, Freya realised. 'I'd better go.' Only that was the problem—she didn't want to go. She wanted to be here with him and she'd never stop wanting him.

The energy between them was undeniable.

How much easier would this all be if she could simply stand up and walk away, instead of looking down at him where he lay?

Zack broke his own 'nowhere near work' rule and his hand went to the back of her head to pull her down to his mouth. The long, slow kiss that evolved she wanted just as much he did. And it blew beyond proportion in a moment as her hand moved down. He put his hand over hers, though not to halt it, and then Freya moved her mouth back from the kiss and licked her lips as she had the night they had met.

She wanted to sink to her knees just as much and just as naturally as she had that first time, and he wanted ten minutes of pleasure to get out of his head.

'Do I stay or go?' She ran a finger along his erection.

'I thought you said you didn't like it?'

'A concession?' Freya smiled.

'Lock the door.'

She got up and did so and as she walked over he went to check in that she was okay with this, because he had pulled back from the two of them last night, Zack knew that. 'Freya—'

'I get it, Zack.'

They did not need a long discussion tonight so

they got back to what they were supposed to be about—sex.

Yet this was different, because Zack never brought it to work and he never just lay there and did nothing except moan with want and relief.

And he could never have known that for Freya this was very different indeed; she had never done this before. She just knelt on the floor and lavished him, loving the pressure of his hand and how he held her hair tight. She took him first with her tongue and then deeper as her hand worked his base.

'More,' Zack moaned, just as she did on occasion, and she took him in as deep as she could and gave him the oblivion he craved.

He sank into bliss and she knelt up higher and her thighs were pressing together at the noises they made, and on the most hellish day and at a less than romantic coupling, they were possibly the closest they had ever been.

Feeling him start to come in her mouth, hearing his shout of relief, Freya came to the salty taste of him.

He made her dizzy.

Her cheek rested on his stomach and she gathered back her breath as Zack lay there. She took it as no insult that his hand slid from her head and he was already asleep.

There was one odd talent Freya had, from too many years hiding in the bathroom, and that was performing a quick tidy up. Freya dealt with all that, she popped it all back and retied his scrubs, then slunk out of his office and sat silent in her own.

And she admitted it properly then.

The life goals she'd had just a short while ago had all shifted.

She was thirty-one years old and, for the first time in her life, Freya was wondering if she was falling in love. Never could she imagine she'd have done what she just had. Zack had no idea that the thought had always made her feel ill.

Not now.

Was this love?

Very possibly, because the thought of him leaving, hurt enough for it to be.

CHAPTER TEN

'THE DONATIONS ARE pouring in,' Freya said to James early on the Saturday after a meeting about Paulo.

It was a reluctant meeting on both their parts.

James had been 'too busy' during the week to touch base, but given the publicity surrounding Paulo, James slotted in a brief catch-up.

Freya didn't want to be there either. It had been a very busy week with work, and Zack aside, the only place Freya now wanted to be was on the back of a horse and letting go some of the tension that she was carrying.

'Donations for the Bright Hope Clinic have started to take off,' Freya said. 'And the general feedback regarding The Hills is positive.'

'General feedback?' James checked.

'As to whether or not the charitable side will

be maintained.' Freya pulled no punches. 'The Hills is high-end luxury and people are waiting to see if it's a gimmick.'

'We'd play with a five-year-old's life as a gimmick?'

'I've pretty much responded with that,' Freya said. 'Still, given that it was such a risky procedure, had it not paid off some people are asking if that would have been it for your foray into charitable work.'

'Well, they don't know me,' James said. 'Still, hopefully not every case will be as complicated. Maria has given her consent to Paulo being photographed, if you could get onto that now.'

'Sure. Will you be in one of the photos?'

'He's not my patient.'

'No, but I'm not going to get Zack to agree. I am working on another angle for him, though. I'm trying to get in touch with an older patient of his—perhaps he'll agree to that—but for now we'll just make it about what's so far been achieved and that's thanks to The Hills partnering with Bright Hope.'

Yes, Freya was tense.

In the absence of Zack, the best photo would be both Mila and James with Paulo, but Freya wasn't game to suggest that!

Things weren't great between them and she guessed now wasn't the time to be asking James about her starting to see her own clients, so instead they finished things up.

'Freya?' James said as she folded up her laptop.

'Yes?'

'I'm still angry.'

'I get that,' Freya snapped, 'but surely you can see that both sides benefit and I happen to care about both sides.'

'I'm not discussing that now,' James said. 'I'm just saying that, even though I'm angry, I'm still your brother and if there's a problem…'

'Problem?' Freya frowned.

'Stephanie said the other that day that you went dizzy.'

'And?' Freya rolled her eyes. 'I knew that she'd make a deal out of it. James, I'd been out all night for New Years Eve. I don't need your concern.'

'Well, like it or not, you've got it.'

'It's not necessary, James. I was ill a long time

ago.' She had been seventeen! James still looked out for her, was still way too overprotective. 'Don't worry, if I need to see someone I'll be sure to ask for a referral.'

So much for leaving it! But that was Freya—once her mind was made up she could not just sit by.

He stared back at her and Freya wondered if he'd got the point she was making so she spelt it out.

'Why don't you have an eating disorder unit here?' Freya asked.

'We can't have everything.'

'Please!' Freya said. 'That's the whole point of The Hills, the patients have everything! Given that the majority of your clientele are in the public eye I'd say an eating disorder unit might be a necessity rather than a luxury. Yet you refer them elsewhere.'

'I'm trying to...' James started, but then he halted and it incensed Freya.

'Trying to watch out for me, trying to avoid hurts, trying to pretend it doesn't exist.'

'You're better now,' James said. 'Do you really need constant reminders?'

They were getting nowhere.

'I need to get on,' Freya said. 'I'll see you up there.' She walked out, collected her camera from her office and headed up to the cardiac unit, where Paulo was now being cared for.

He looked amazing.

The dusky colour of his skin on admission was now a gorgeous coffee colour and his lips were pink and he was sucking on an ice stick.

And then Zack came in with a colleague he was handing Paulo over to, to check on the boy before he headed off on a well-deserved week-end break.

'I thought you were off for the weekend!' Maria exclaimed.

'In an hour I shall be,' Zack said, and then looked at Paulo. 'I don't have to ask how you are, do I?' He glanced over and nodded to James and saw Freya and her damned camera. 'Is Maria okay with this?'

'Maria is,' Freya said.

'I'm delighted to have our picture taken if it

will do some good.' Maria nodded. 'Will you be in it?'

'No, thanks.' Zack shook his head. 'I keep it up here, Maria.'

'Come on, Zack.' Maria was the one who pushed for him to join in the happy shot.

'Seriously.' Zack shook his head. 'Maria, I've got to go and see another patient now.' He was honest. 'They don't need my smiling thumbs up if it doesn't go well for them.'

It was who he was, Freya thought.

Private.

And she wanted in, though she was doing her best to hold back.

Zack went and wrote up his notes and his instructions for Paulo and his other patients while he was away.

He had a small baby on NICU that had already had more tests and procedures done than most people had in a lifetime but he had to go back up there now and order some more before he made a decision next week as to whether or not to operate.

'Hey,' Zack said, when Freya came out from the photo shoot. 'Are we still on for riding?'

'We're at work!' she reminded him.

'Sorry.' He rolled his eyes. 'I've got cabin fever. I've been here since Tuesday.'

'I've booked us for midday,' Freya said. 'We can meet there.' She gave him the address and Zack nodded.

She had meant what she'd said, Zack thought, about today having no strings attached.

Their paths had only crossed briefly since the other night.

For Zack it still felt like it had been a bit of a dream. Even when she had come in to wake him up when PICU had paged him a couple of hours later, Freya had made no reference to what had taken place.

He had brought them to work and the trouble for Zack was that he wasn't adequately troubled by it.

Even now he had asked her about riding, and there were people around.

He needed to reel things back, but it was very hard to do so when you were walking through stables and another person had come up with the very thing you needed.

It felt so good to get away and be doing something he probably wouldn't have made the time for today.

'I didn't know how experienced you were,' Freya said when he arrived. 'I said intermediate...'

Oh, no, he wasn't.

It didn't take long to establish that Zack knew his way around horses and he was given Bullet, who, Zack was assured, lived up to his name.

Freya had Camp, her usual horse, who was patient and steady and everything that she was not.

And they were off.

Together but separate and it suited Freya today. Half an hour in, Zack found a lovely flat length and went for a gallop as Freya just plodded along and looked at the stunning view, past the city and out to the Pacific Ocean.

Then she heard Zack coming back and he was all breathless and Bullet wasn't even sweating.

'I needed that,' Zack said, falling into pace with her.

'And I needed this,' Freya sighed.

After a while they stopped to eat the lunch Freya had made. It was nice to breathe in fresh air and eat but Freya was distracted. Her mind kept going over that morning and her conversation with James.

'You okay?' Zack checked.

'I will be,' Freya said. 'I had words with James.'

And they weren't anonymous strangers any more and this wasn't about Mila and James so she told him the part she felt she wanted to, even if it was rare that she spoke about it.

'James took on a lot when I was ill and now we can hardly talk about it.' She told him how he'd come and hauled her out of a nightclub and that she'd collapsed. How James had found a rehab place for her that was a bit alternative but which had suited her.

'How long were you there for?' Zack asked.

'Six months. Two of those were spent fighting.'

'Fighting?'

'Well, pretending I agreed with them while waiting for an opportunity to do another hundred sit-ups... And I loathed group discussions.

Anyway, finally I saw the damage I was doing to myself, that I'd already done, and I decide to work on getting well. They didn't believe me at first. They thought I was just going through the motions to get out.'

'I'm not with you.'

'Well, I just made a decision without all the drama and crying and pouring out my fears. I just set a goal—to get well. So, yes, two months fighting, four months starting to get well and then a lifetime of keeping to it.'

'Is it a fight every day?' He was curious.

'Some days,' Freya said. 'James wants it cured, fixed, healed, and in many ways it is. I'll never go back to how I was.' Freya was sure of it. 'I know that. I just need healthier ways of dealing with tension. My parents said I was attention-seeking...'

'Were you?'

'Not at first,' Freya said. 'I was actually trying to get away from attention. My parents' divorce was everywhere, all their lovers were speaking out, and it was horrific. I know you think I'll go to any lengths for publicity but I'm nowhere close to them. They spoke not just about the rows and the money but about their sex lives, and their lovers did too.'

He said nothing and she was so glad.

'It was excruciating,' Freya admitted. 'I turned to food.' She told him about the reports about her being only a little younger and a whole lot larger than her father's latest girlfriend. 'I was a teenager and there were pictures of my stomach and thighs everywhere. I lost some weight and I lost it quickly, but instead of stopping I carried on, and then maybe I did get some attention from my mother...'

Freya thought back. 'Not for long, though. And so I'd go to clubs and drink and get into trouble and then sit at home and watch an interview my mother might be having about how hard it was to have a troubled teenager. And then I had my father, when I collapsed, on the one hand asking the press to respect the family's privacy while on the other getting off with some nineteen-year-old, knowing the press would erupt.' She still could not stand the memories. 'Everyone knew my business, or thought they did,' Freya said, 'but

I had a bigger secret and I was on a mission by then—to get below a hundred pounds.'

'You met that goal?'

'I knocked that goal into the ground and kept going,' Freya sighed. 'James was beside himself. I think he was the only one in my family with any sense at that time.'

'You're usually close to your brother?'

'When we're not arguing.' Freya smiled.

They lay there for ages and then looked at the map. 'I'm going to take the long way back,' Zack said. 'And go fast.'

'I'll take the short way and go slowly.'

They met back at their cars, all dirty and smelly and worn out from the bliss of a day away from it all.

'Do you want to go and grab dinner?' Zack offered.

'No, I want to go home and shower and get changed,' Freya said. 'And then eat.' She deliberately didn't invite him this time but the very last place Freya wanted to be was back at the hotel.

She was tired of putting on the same clothes

in the morning, tired of her hair smelling of the lemon ginger hotel shampoo.

It smelt fantastic on Zack, she just didn't want it on her.

Freya liked her own things and if he didn't want a part of them that was up to Zack.

'Sounds good,' Zack said. 'I'll see you there.'

And Freya did her very best as she got into her car, and drove off, not to look for a deeper meaning.

CHAPTER ELEVEN

FREYA LOST ZACK on the freeway and she stopped off at a store to get something more suitable for a tall, muscled male who had been riding than anything she had in her fridge, so he was already outside her place when she arrived.

Red was leaving the building as she got out of her car. 'Been riding?' he asked with a cheerful smile.

'Yes.' Freya smiled back. 'Red, this is Zack.'

'Hi, Red.'

Zack watched as Freya and Red chatted for a couple of moments. 'We're all getting together next Friday,' Red said. 'Are you in?'

'I'm in.' Freya nodded. 'I'll see you then.'

They walked up the stairs to her apartment and Zack was surprised when Freya opened the door and a small dog wagged her tail from the sofa and Freya went over and made a huge fuss of her.

'You have a dog?'

'I do,' Freya said. 'Her name is Cleo and she's a very old lady.'

It really was a home, Zack thought as he looked around. It was large, open-plan and very tidy, as he might have expected from Freya, but the dog he hadn't expected.

'Who lets her out when you stay with me?'

'Red or another of the neighbours…we all help out. Cleo's too old to go to a boarding kennel now.'

'You all get on?'

'We do,' Freya said. 'We try and get together once a month and have a barbecue or something.'

She had a life, a very, very nice life.

'I'm going first,' Freya said. 'Help yourself to a drink.'

'First?'

'I want a shower.'

And Zack got the hint that she wanted to shower alone and if he wanted a beer he'd better start liking the American stuff.

He sat out on a large balcony that looked towards the hills that they'd ridden in and it was actually nice to sit out on a balcony that didn't have one above and one below.

Freya rinsed off a whole day of riding and used her own shampoo and conditioner and soap.

She stepped out and, even with a steamy mirror, a very self-aware Freya frowned at her reflection.

She had spent way too much time examining her body but it was for different reasons that she examined it now.

Wiping her mirror with her towel, she saw the pink of her breasts and the swell of them.

She might be getting her occasional period, Freya thought, but then glanced at the packet of pills she had been taking since the second night in his hotel room.

And then she put it out of her mind.

It was nice to be able to open a drawer and pull on some yoga pants and a top rather than scrabble on the floor for last night's clothes.

And, she decided as she combed her hair and tied it back, if she went to the hotel again, next time she was going to bring some things.

He might choose to live out of luggage.

Not she.

'Do you need a hand?' Zack called as she came into the kitchen.

'No, thanks.'

Freya grilled two steaks, one massive, one smaller, and she made a large salad. He watched her measuring everything out when he'd have just thrown it in.

Two spoons of oil, one of vinegar, a quarter of a teaspoon of salt.

And she could feel him watching her from the balcony but she wasn't going to change her routines for him.

She carried them out and he got the massive steak and she and Cleo shared the smaller one.

'I'm going to ache tomorrow,' Freya said. 'It's been ages since I rode. I should try and get around to it more often.'

'And me,' Zack said. 'It's been great. I'm so glad I didn't give it up.'

'Why would you give it up?'

'My brother was killed in a riding accident. You know how they say get back on the horse…'

'Zack!' Freya was appalled. 'This must bring up some—'

'Freya, it does and it doesn't. I love riding; I miss that part of home. I don't spend my life avoiding thinking about my brother. It's there every day, the same way your eating disorder is. Sometimes it's hard, sometimes not so much, but it's a part of your past that has to live with the you of today.'

It was always there, a part of her past that could never be erased.

The fattest pug he had ever seen looked up at him. 'Not a chance,' Zack said, but cut off a piece.

'Don't give it to her,' Freya said. 'She's already had some.'

'How old is she?'

'Thirteen,' Freya said. 'James got her for me when I came out of rehab.'

'Did it help?'

'Very much,' Freya said. 'I didn't have Red and a group of neighbours then and dogs don't forget mealtimes...' She looked at Cleo and she could hear her heavy breathing. 'I don't think I'll have her for much longer. Still, the vet says that if she loses some weight it will help with her joints. I can't imagine my life without her.' And then she shook her head. 'Sorry.'

'For what?'

'We've been talking about you losing a brother…'

'Freya,' Zack said. 'Losing Cleo will hurt.'

'Yes,' she said. 'James thinks I should get another puppy before she dies.' She rolled her eyes.

'Are you going to tell me what's going on between you and James?'

'I told you.'

'You two haven't been talking since before this morning.'

She looked at Zack and Freya was confused. She was handing over more and more of her life, yet she wanted to.

Freya trusted him, she knew nothing would go further than them.

'When we were growing up, as dysfunctional as it was, my parents were involved in a lot of overseas charities. They'd take James and me along for photoshoots and things but a lot of good was done. James pours everything into The Hills and it annoyed me that there was no charitable side to it. He avoids that sort of thing.'

'A lot of people do.'

'Not James,' Freya said. 'And last year we had a discussion and he said if I found the right charity and handled all the PR side of it, he'd implement it. Anyway, I didn't have to look far. I already knew about Bright Hope. My good friend Mila runs it.'

'I met her when I saw Paulo,' Zack said. 'Actually, there's another patient she wants me to review. She seems nice. Very dedicated.'

'She's James's ex,' Freya said.

'Oh! I see.'

'Believe me, you don't. She and I have remained friends. I just told James that Mila's the founder of Bright Hope.'

'How could he not have known?'

'Because the reason he avoids anything that combines medicine and aid work is because Mila is so heavily involved in it. She works overseas but she came back and started the foundation...'

'Was it a bad break-up?'

'The worst,' Freya said. 'He jilted her on their wedding day.'

Oh, there were so many reasons Freya didn't trust people.

She loved her brother very much but still had no idea how he could have done that to Mila, or why.

'Families!' Zack said.

'We all have them.' Freya shrugged. 'Even if we choose not to deal with them.'

He heard the slight dig.

'I'm going back in April,' Zack reminded her.

'I know. How's the baby doing?' she asked.

'He collapsed in the ambulance on the way to Brisbane. Cale said that they got to him just in time. But he's doing okay. He'll need more surgery when he's older, but fairly minor.'

'What does your dad say?'

'We haven't spoken about it.'

'You haven't spoken about it?'

'Freya...' He went to get another beer. 'Do you want one?'

'No, I just keep them there for Red if he comes to keep Cleo company.'

'Do you want—?'

'Nothing,' she said. She was actually incredibly tired but curious about Zack. 'Do you help out when you go back?'

'Help out?'

'With your father's practice.'

'I don't stay there long enough for that,' Zack admitted. 'You know how you said you couldn't stand everyone knowing your business—that's what home's like,' he explained. 'Everyone knows everything and it's great for some, but not for me. I swear I could not get out of that place fast enough. I used to come back in my breaks but it just got harder and harder to after Toby died. He'd worked in the family practice so his dying left a big hole, not just for his family.'

'On the community?'

Zack nodded.

'One they think you should fill?'

'They can't get another doctor, it all falls on my dad. As well as the fact I don't want to settle down and give them grandchildren. Toby was married and Alice wanted babies, and by now...'

'So if your brother had lived?'

'He didn't, though,' Zack said. 'But, yes, they seem to think that had he lived…' Zack didn't tell her the rest. 'Anyway, it's not the life for me.'

'What is?'

'What I've got,' Zack said. 'A few weeks here, a few months there.'

'Why can't a few months be *there* to give your father a break?'

Zack didn't answer.

'I still don't get why you'd choose a hotel over an apartment.'

'It suits me.' Zack said.

'Company on tap,' Freya said, and was cross with herself for the jealous note to her voice. She couldn't knock it as that was how they'd met after all.

Zack said nothing and Freya got up and sorted out the plates, which had Cleo wake up, suddenly interested. Freya knew why—he had saved some steak and thought she didn't notice when he sneaked it to Cleo.

'I'm going to take her for her little walk,' Freya said.

'I'll clear up.'

She was suddenly unsettled.

Freya carried Cleo down the stairs and took her for her little nightly outing and was, despite a wonderful day and one of the nicest evenings, very, very close to tears.

He didn't deny that his life was the life for him.

Zack didn't make excuses about his ways with women.

She wished, in some ways, that it had stayed at one night.

One amazing night instead of a very intense glimpse of a future that Freya now wanted but could never have.

She'd been snarky.

It had been but a few weeks and already she was counting down the days left to her, or biting her tongue to stop herself from suggesting he ditch the hotel and stay with her instead.

He'd decline, Freya knew.

And that was just as well because imagine having three months of bliss and…

Two months.

January would be over soon.

'I'm going to be without both of you soon, aren't

I?' In the darkness all she could see was Cleo's pink tongue and her fur baby was out of breath from the shortest walk. 'You'd better be here when he goes,' Freya warned Cleo. 'I'm going to need you so much.' And then she picked Cleo up and buried her face in her fur. 'I'm so selfish...' Freya said, but she had to tell her friend. 'Cleo, I think I'm pregnant.'

Cleo just carried on breathing. Just kissed her face and cuddled in till Freya's panic subsided.

'I can't be,' Freya said to Cleo, who really didn't care if she was or not.

She just loved her back.

Freya carried Cleo back up the stairs and put her on the sofa with her toy. The kitchen was tidy and Freya could hear Zack in the shower and it hurt that it felt so nice to turn off the lights and get into bed and know that he'd join her.

Zack wasn't sure that he would.

Here was everything he had always avoided and possibly with good reason because it made him want more.

He should get dressed and go, Zack thought.

Cleo had got off the sofa and was crying at

the bedroom door, and Zack grinned when he came out.

'I'm sleeping in her bed.'

'Yes, and she'll hate you for it, even if you did sneak her some steak. Did you have pets?'

'A few,' Zack said, and got into bed and tried not to think of home.

'I'm going to start seeing clients,' Freya said. 'I haven't told James yet, but I'm going to.'

'Good.'

'I was thinking about it while we were riding.'

'I was thinking too,' Zack said.

'About?'

He didn't answer. Zack just lay there thinking about plans that had been made and might be broken. He was tired, not physically, though. For the first time he was tired of hotels and starting over, of borrowing a horse, leasing a car, starting out, over and over again…

He wanted this but did not want it, just as he wanted home but not to be there.

Life was easier with no names.

Except *she* had one and, lying in the dark,

he told Freya what he hadn't been able to over dinner.

'I stay away because I'm worried that I might end up telling them that Toby wasn't happy when he died,' Zack said.

He'd told no one.

Ever.

'We'd gone camping for a weekend,' Zack said. 'I was surprised when he suggested it but we just went out into the bush. It was great...'

Actually, no, it hadn't been. It had been revealing.

'He told me how unhappy he was,' Zack said, and Freya looked at him.

'He'd been going out with Alice since they were teenagers and she'd stuck by him while he'd gone off and studied medicine. He said that he'd had enough and wanted to move to the city. So when I am home I get to hear how happy Toby was, what a great son, husband, doctor, and how happy he'd been there and how he'd hate how I've let them down. I dread that one day I'll tell the truth: that he was planning on getting out...'

'He was going to leave his wife?'

Zack nodded.

What a terrible secret to carry, Freya thought, to be the only one to know and be able to say nothing.

'That was why he'd asked me to go camping with him. He wanted my take on things.'

'And that was?'

'I had lots of takes on it,' Zack said, and he told her about that last night. 'Never knowing that the next day he'd be dead.'

'Was he killed outright?'

'No. At first I didn't think it was that serious,' Zack said, but then he shook his head. 'Actually, I think I did know because I activated the locator beacon and you only do that if things are dire. And then it was a matter of waiting.' The longest wait ever. 'I love the outback,' Zack said. 'You have never seen anywhere more beautiful and the remoteness is hard to comprehend, but it's a long wait if someone you love is dying.'

'How long?'

'Four hours,' Zack said. 'Well, three spent dying, one hour with him dead. I told him I'd live for both of us…'

And he had.
Zack crammed everything in.
Then he corrected himself in his head.
He had crammed everything in bar a relationship.

CHAPTER TWELVE

FREYA SLEPT WITH the windows open.

For everything Zack liked about hotels, windows that didn't open were one of the things that he didn't like. It was a cool night and the sound of rain was lulling.

Not for Freya.

She lay listening to the sound of night-time from her bed but with Zack by her side, and all in her world was shaken.

Beautifully so but scarily so.

And how could you let yourself simply enjoy something when you'd been told it couldn't last?

And what if what she had discussed earlier with Cleo turned out to be right?

'What's wrong?' Zack asked, as Freya turned to get comfortable again.

'Nothing,' she said.

'Liar.' He gave her a kiss. 'But that's okay.'

Side on they faced each other and Freya found that she was smiling. 'You smell of my soap.'

'I taste of your soap,' Zack said. 'If you need to check.' His leg hooked her in closer and he made her feel all shivery as his hand played with one tender breast. 'For someone who doesn't like it…'

'I didn't like the idea of it,' Freya said. 'I'd never done it.'

Zack frowned.

'So in my office…'

'It was my first time.'

They'd never spoken about it. Sometimes, for Zack, it almost felt like a dream, only he knew that it hadn't been. It had been the night they'd moved their relationship into work. They'd shifted the lines but in ways he hadn't even known at the time.

That should daunt him. No doubt it would soon—that something that was clearly an issue for her wasn't when she was with him. Zack had thought oral the least intimate of sex, but not now.

He slipped his hand between her legs and got the clamp of her thighs.

'I don't think I'd like it.'

'Do you want to try?'

Freya nodded.

Her mind was going at a hundred miles an hour. She wanted everything while she had him. Always she stopped him, beneath the belly button a no-go zone for that beautiful mouth and she didn't really know why.

'I'm messed up, aren't I?' Freya said.

'I told you the day I met you, that's how I want you.'

It hadn't been what he'd meant then but it made her smile now. He kissed her long and deep until her thighs were loose to his hand. And then he moved down and her breasts were so tender, and Freya was starting to know why.

Zack was oblivious, blissfully so. He just heard her fevered moans as he tasted and sucked and licked till she rolled from her side to her back.

He slid down and paid the same attention to her stomach and then he moved lower and kissed her right up her thighs, nibbling at the top inner part that she had once hated so much.

Zack made her body feel beautiful, every part

of it. She had worked on herself for ever and had got to like herself enough, but he made her in love with it.

'I don't like it,' Freya said when his mouth took possession, and he ignored her and probed at the tension, tasting her deep, and then back to her clitoris. Freya closed her thighs on his head and he burrowed in deeper and her hips lifted from the bed. She resisted the pleasure, she stayed tight to his tongue, and then Zack moaned into her.

She felt the vibration, the sensual moan of his want and his turn-on. His focus was intent now and she succumbed. It was the most bliss she had known, to come to the most intimate kiss his mouth could give, to be tasted and adored.

There was no triumphant smile as his mouth lifted, Zack was the one crossing his own lines now. He came up the bed and kissed her mouth as deeply as he had her sex. He had Freya taste herself on his lips, his cheeks, and then he moaned again as he slid in. The same moan he had given earlier, and they stopped holding back because this wasn't just sex.

'I'm going to come,' Zack said, almost with regret, because he was loving her, he knew.

Freya was frantic, coming, while making this strange attempt to climb out of arms that would one day let her go. They were saying each other's names, breathing, kissing, coming and so close, so completely besotted and not fighting it now.

'Zack…' She pressed her lips together because she was going to say the wrong thing and lay there afterwards, with something else building— tears. The utter release to her body, the clearing of her mind and she was as close to crying as she dared to be.

He held her so hard afterwards. 'You can cry,' Zack said.

But she wouldn't.

He'd had everything, all of her, he had taken her right to the edge. She would not give him that.

CHAPTER THIRTEEN

'WHY DON'T YOU ditch the hotel?' Freya said.

She shouldn't have.

It was six a.m. and they lay chatting in the dark, talking about, of all things, his suits.

'How much can you get into a backpack?' Freya had asked. And then she'd found out he bought suits and that, when he moved on, he donated them.

'It's an expensive wardrobe.'

'Yeah, well, it's an up-to-date one.'

And then he'd admitted that living out of a backpack was tiring at times, and had been about to say he was actually looking forward to going home for a few weeks, when someone, namely Freya, who had to fix everything this very minute, suggested he move in.

'Freya,' he half groaned in frustration.

'I'm not asking you to move in as in live together, just…' She could have kicked herself.

Zack just lay there.

'Forget it,' Freya said. 'I was just thinking out loud.'

She simply could not stop thinking.

About them.

'I'm going to take Cleo out.'

Freya stood in her dressing gown and she was too embarrassed to even admit to Cleo what she'd just said to Zack.

'It's not such a stupid idea,' Freya said hopefully to her friend, but then gave in.

Oh, it was such a stupid idea and, of all things, to say it on the first night that he'd come back to her apartment.

Freya was worried, though.

The clock was ticking on them and not only couldn't she imagine him gone, Freya was rather worried that there might be a more permanent reason for them to keep in touch.

She felt sick.

Not a nervous sick feeling, more there was a

taste in her mouth as she came back into the apartment.

Cleo waddled into the bedroom and Zack lay there with his hands behind his head as she jumped up onto the bed.

He *was* leaving LA at the end of his three months.

He looked around the bedroom and he knew that he needed to head back to the hotel.

'Hi.' Freya came in, trying desperately to detract from the prior conversation. 'I just got an email...' Zack blinked, he was just waking up but Freya was in busy mode. 'Do you remember when you were in Canada a few years back and that hockey player went into cardiac arrest...'

Zack nodded. 'Why?'

'Well, I was just trying for a new angle. I get that you don't want to be photographed with kids, but he's here in LA and I thought we could get the two of you together.'

'Freya,' Zack said, sitting up, 'how many ways can I say it? I don't want to be a part of your publicity stunts. I'll do the surgery—'

'It's just such a great opportunity.'

'I don't get involved, Freya, they don't owe me anything. I do my best for them in Theatre, without obligation. I don't want to be making small talk with some guy who had the misfortune to go into cardiac arrest in front of ten thousand people and now has to feel he needs to publicly thank me for doing my job.'

Freya gave a tight shrug. 'Just trying to do mine.'

'It's Sunday,' he pointed out. 'And I only get one off a month.'

'Sure.' Freya nodded. 'Do you want some breakfast? I'm just making some.'

'A coffee would be great.'

He lay back on the bed again. She'd be in soon with a needle and thread to try and hem him in.

Cleo waddled up to his chest and stared at him with her big pug eyes and he stroked her head and thought, What the hell am I doing?

He'd told her stuff last night that he could never have envisaged telling another, he had made love, and Zack had not lied with his mouth, he'd adored her.

It was all too close, and that was the very thing he avoided.

He didn't want to be tied down like his brother had been, or chained to a town as his father was. They were getting far too close and another couple of months of this and, Zack wasn't stupid, his leaving was going to hurt her.

And no hurt had ever been intended.

It was time to call it now, Zack knew, before they got in any deeper than they were.

Cleo bared her teeth.

She just stared him down and bared her teeth and it was as if she warned him, in or out?

'Cleo!' Freya threatened from the kitchen when she heard her growl. She went to make coffee but found she had none. Coffee wasn't something she drank but she generally kept some in case of company.

She added it to the list she kept on her phone and divided the drink she'd blended into two glasses as the toast popped up. For the first time in the kitchen she was distracted. Freya had bigger problems on her mind than food for once, and instead of preparing just one plate she made two plates and smeared on some avocado she'd mashed and added a shake of black pepper.

She would go and get a pregnancy kit today and get this over and done with. Maybe when she'd found out it was a false alarm she could relax. Freya carried the tray into the bedroom. 'I was thinking, maybe today we...' And then she stopped because Zack was sitting on the edge of the bed with his jeans and boots on and he was pulling on his T-shirt.

'I need to get back to the hotel,' Zack said. 'There's some work I need—'

'It's Sunday,' Freya pointed out, just as he had.

'Yep.'

'Have some breakfast.'

'I don't generally eat breakfast, and definitely not green ones.' He was direct, he was honest and, yes, it hurt a lot. 'It's all too much, Freya.'

'Zack—'

'Freya, I made it clear. I don't want a relationship, I don't want someone making plans for my day off, I don't want to have to account—'

'You're annoyed because I suggested you move out of the hotel.'

'A bit,' Zack said. 'Do you know why I like it there, Freya?' He looked at the tray she'd prepared. 'If I ask for coffee, I get coffee. When I put the "Do not disturb" sign on the door, guess what? They don't disturb...'

They weren't talking about coffee or signs on the door, Freya knew.

Zack didn't want more than sex. He'd been upfront from the start and she had been more than willing to go along with it.

It was Freya whose wants had changed.

And he told himself that on the drive back to the hotel.

Last night had been amazing—dinner, conversation and the sex had been amazing.

More than amazing.

He wanted to turn the hired car around and go back there. He wanted to have a decent row with Freya and tell her to get out of fixing and sorting mode and get back to bed.

Zack got back to the hotel, went up in the elevator and then passed the maid with her trolley, doling out the toiletries so that five hundred guests smelt the same.

Then he stepped into the room that had been beautifully serviced and he thought about heading out for the day. Just driving into the hills, or taking a walk along the beach.

He needed a shower, he smelt of sex, or rather he smelt of Freya.

Zack did everything on his to-do list. He showered, changed and then headed for the hills, and that evening, instead of the hotel bar, he took a walk on the beach and told himself that this was the life he had chosen. And he had chosen it carefully. He never wanted to be tied down, or have people reliant on or beholden to him.

Not his patients—he fixed what he could and let them get on with their lives.

Not his family—they all knew how that had worked out.

And certainly he did not need someone who decided what he might want to eat for breakfast!

Damned cheek, Zack decided, and headed back to the hotel.

He went to the bar because it really was *that* easy, only it wasn't so easy tonight because he didn't want company.

Only his own.

Back up to his room he went and the bed had been turned down, the towels and soaps all replaced, and Zack found himself kicking his backpack across the room.

CHAPTER FOURTEEN

IT HURT.

Far, far more than the end of any other relation-ship ever had.

Even though Zack would insist that it hadn't been a relationship because he didn't do that type of thing.

'Men!' Freya said to Cleo as they stood in the little patch of garden early one morning, more than a week after their row.

She carried her back up the stairs and, instead of driving to work, Freya decided that she would run. She hadn't run all week, she'd been huddled on the sofa at night with Cleo and busy with work by day.

It was time to get back on track with her sched-ules. She had a change of clothes at work so she pulled on her running gear and put in her earphones and did what she loved to do. She arrived at work all hot and sweaty and stood bent over in the stunning foyer.

'James will have you using the side entrance,' Zack said as he went past, and Freya actually laughed.

She wasn't the prettiest sight for such expensive surroundings but she felt better for a run and glad that she and Zack were almost at the point they could acknowledge each other in passing.

There was a meeting with James this morning and Zack would be there so Freya wasn't looking forward to it one bit.

She walked into the changing rooms and they were like a luxury spa. There was soft music and fluffy towels and Freya stepped under the delicious jets of water, and then everything shifted.

Her legs started to shake and Freya went dizzy. She didn't even turn off the taps, she just stepped out and grabbed at a towel then sat on the bench with her head down.

'Freya?'

She could hear Stephanie's voice and it seemed

to be coming from a long way off, except her face was right next to her ear.

'I'm okay,' Freya said.

'You're ever so white.'

'I just need a moment,' Freya said. 'Could you get me some tea?'

The waiting rooms all had oolong tea, kept warm by a candle, and little glasses and so it was just a couple of moments before Stephanie returned.

By then Freya had put on a robe and was a bit more together. 'Sorry about that,' she said.

'It's fine.' Stephanie smiled. 'I saw that you ran in. Maybe you overdid it.'

'Maybe,' Freya said, and she felt a twist of indignation because she knew the implication behind Stephanie's words. She had, in fact, underdone things this week but it was always there, the feeling that everyone was waiting for her to slide back into ways of old.

Even James, Freya thought.

They made no mention of her past, it was a subject he avoided, but she could always see the concern in his eyes.

She didn't need it.

And it was one of the things she had loved about Zack. He hadn't raised his eyes at her ways, he had let her be, and she missed him so much.

So much.

Over and over she tried to tell herself it had just been a few weeks, that you couldn't fall in love in that time, and certainly it wasn't love if it was unrequited.

'I'm fine now,' Freya said, and put down the little cup but she knew she was going to throw up. 'Honestly.'

Please, go now, she thought.

Freya walked to the toilet and closed the door and she wished Stephanie would leave as she threw up the tea as quietly as she could.

No, Freya thought, she hadn't overdone her run—the nausea and dizzy spells were for different reasons altogether.

How the hell could she ever tell Zack that she was pregnant?

Freya put on her grey dress with capped sleeves and did her hair and make-up and then she had another glass of tea and that one was nice.

Feeling a whole lot better, she arrived at the meeting room.

'Where's Zack?'

'He's talking to your good friend Mila about another patient.'

Freya ignored the dig and James got down to business and said he would, as of today, be starting to put out the feelers for a new cardiac surgeon to replace Zack. 'Already?'

'Well, if they have to give notice. I just asked Zack if he'd go on a month-to-month contract but he said no, he's out of here at the end of March.

'And it's February today.' James said.

So it was.

'Morning.' Zack came into the meeting room with no apologies for being late and she and James shared a small smile.

He was such an arrogant bastard.

Even down to the fact they were having this meeting in a meeting room when usually they'd be in James's office for such things.

Zack played second fiddle to no one.

'I can't stay long,' Zack said. 'I've got a patient that's not doing well on NICU.'

'I heard,' James said. 'Are you going to operate?'

'I don't know. I've just spoken with Mila and we're trying to schedule Bright Hope patients. I want to squeeze an ablation onto the end of the Sunday list on the fourteenth.'

'That's Valentine's Day.' James raised an eyebrow. 'Won't you want to be finishing up early?'

'Same as any other day to me,' Zack responded. 'I'm an incurable unromantic.'

James took a call and it would seem that it was a personal one because he excused himself and took it outside the office, leaving Freya bristling beside Zack.

'Can you not do that?'

'What?'

'Consistently point out…' She was so incensed. 'I get you don't do romance but your little digs are unnecessary.'

'I wasn't digging, Freya.' Zack gave a bored eye-roll at her drama. 'I've used the same line for ten years. I'm not changing *anything* for your benefit.'

That was a dig at the breakfast she'd made him.

Oh, yes, it was because there was a small smirk on his lips as she opened her mouth to argue.

Then she closed it and then, to hell with it, she said it. 'I'd run out of coffee.'

'What on earth are you talking about?' Zack asked.

He knew full well!

'You overthink everything,' he said.

'No, I don't.'

They were sulking and turned on and now staring ahead as they sniped, and both wanted to be down on the floor.

He had told James with absolute certainty that he would not be staying on after March, but the certainty had been in his voice only.

'Freya.' James came back into the meeting room and his voice had them both turn around. 'That was Red.'

'Red?' Freya frowned. 'Why would he call you?'

'Because he can't get through on your phone.'

Red had James's number in case Freya was away and there was an emergency.

'He thinks you ought to go home. Cleo's not well,' James told her. 'I'll drive you.'

'I don't need you to drive me,' Freya snapped, and got up. 'I can drive myself.'

But she'd run to work this morning.

'What's going on?' Zack asked James when Freya had left, as if he didn't know, as if just last week a fat pug hadn't been asleep on his feet and then stood on his chest, baring her teeth at him.

'Her dog's not well,' James said. 'She's a vicious little thing.'

Freya or Cleo? Zack nearly said, but stopped himself. It was getting harder and harder to separate things, and he was glad when James gave up on the meeting.

'Can we do this tomorrow?' James asked.

'I'm in Theatre all day tomorrow.'

'Well, I've got a list this evening.' James was distracted and so too was Zack. 'We'll work out a time later.'

'Will she be okay?' Zack asked.

'Cleo?' James said, and Zack frowned as if he had no idea who James was talking about. 'Oh, you mean Freya. I think so, though you never really know with Freya. She always says that she's fine.'

Zack found her coming out of the changing room, where Freya had left her phone.

'You haven't got your car,' Zack said. 'Do you want me to drive you?'

'No, thank you,' Freya said. 'You're busy today. I'll get Stephanie to call for a car.'

Stephanie did so. 'Are you still not feeling well?' she enquired, and Freya wished she was more like Zack and simply didn't answer questions that she didn't want to.

'I'm much better. Thanks for all your help this morning,' Freya said. 'I just got a call and my dog's sick.'

'Cleo?'

'Yes.'

Freya knew that Red wouldn't call without good reason and she was right.

The vet was there and Cleo lay on the sofa and her little tail thumped when she saw Freya.

'She got all breathless,' Red said, and then the vet told her things weren't going to get better.

'She's comfortable. We can take her back to the clinic and put her on some diuretics…'

'No.' Freya shook her head. 'She hates being away from here.' It was why she didn't put her in boarding kennels and why she'd be grateful forever to Red because in the last year of an old dog's life she'd stayed home every night.

It was time, but not for Freya.

'Can I have a day with her?' Freya asked. 'Can you do it here?'

'I'll come by with Kathy at the end of surgery,' he said, and Freya nodded. Kathy was her favourite nurse at the vet's.

She thanked the vet and she thanked Red and saw them all out, and then she sat on the sofa with her best friend who'd seen her so far on her journey.

'I'm not getting another puppy,' Freya told her. 'I could never love it as much as you.' She buried her face in Cleo's black fur. 'And I don't think it would be very fair on the baby.' She looked into loving black eyes. 'Shall we find out?'

Poor Cleo had been listening to her rabbit on

about it for days now and it didn't seem very fair that she died not knowing for sure.

And so she peed on the stick and came out a few moments later.

'I am,' she said to Cleo, and she accepted her lick and gave Cleo a kiss as the news sank in.

She was pregnant by a man who had hauled on his boots at the first sniff of commitment.

A man she was seriously head over heels about.

But more than that.

She was pregnant.

But more than that...

Freya wanted to be.

Zack knew that James had an evening theatre list and he actually drove past Freya's and wondered if he should go up.

It was odd, but when James had said that Cleo was vicious, Zack had wanted to laugh. That morning, back in her bed, he'd thought Cleo had been warning him to be nice to her mistress. Instead, it had just been a demented dog.

It was her demented dog, though, who had been with her through all the hard times. He saw Freya come down the stairs, carrying Cleo and chatting to her as she did her business and then back up the stairs they went.

And a little while later he saw a couple come down carrying a bundle in a blanket and he knew it was the vet and assistant and that Cleo had just been euthanised.

Zack, who never got close to anyone, was tearing up over a dog, or was it over Freya and how devastated she must feel right now?

This would not end up in bed, Zack told himself as he got out of the car. He was knocking on a door as a friend.

Or maybe it would end in bed, he amended, but only if she so chose.

Yet the woman who answered it didn't just surprise him—Freya shocked him.

'Yes?'

She was pale and rather angry looking but what floored Zack was that she was absolutely dry-eyed.

'I heard that your dog wasn't well...'

'And?'

'Freya?'

'What do you want, Zack?' Freya asked. 'Do you think sex is going to help?' She looked at him. 'You do, don't you?'

'I get what works for me might not for you. I'm just checking if you're okay.'

'Well, as you can see, I am.'

She slammed the door on him.

Screw you, Freya thought.

Oh, she wanted him but, more than that, she wanted Cleo tonight.

Her phone buzzed and it was a text from Mila.

James told me about Cleo.

Then it buzzed again and it was James.

Do you want me to stop by?

No, thanks, I'm fine.

How many ways could she say it?

Red came and drank all her beer and he cried and then he did all the stuff with the bowls and leads and things for her.

And finally a teary Red headed off and it left

Freya alone in her apartment minus Cleo, and that had never happened before.

She'd done everything right by her, Freya told herself. Cleo had had the best possible last day.

There was only one thing about this day Freya regretted.

That Zack wasn't there.

Not for the sex, or the possible progression of them, and not because she had found out she was pregnant...

It would have helped to have him here tonight.

Just that.

CHAPTER FIFTEEN

IT WAS THE oddest week.

No Cleo to chat to.

All her routines felt shot and she didn't know how to tell Zack the news.

Beth had returned from her honeymoon and they had a girls' night in to go through the photos and videos.

The tamest girls' night in—they were all pregnant now, not that Freya let on.

She was detoxing too, she told them!

'The photos are amazing,' Beth said. 'Except these ones.'

There was Zack striding down the stairs and people turning and frowning in annoyance as he messed up the shot.

And Freya found herself laughing quietly and said that she wanted a copy.

'I can have the crowd edited out,' Beth offered.
The crowd being her friends!
'No, no,' Freya said. 'I like it.'
So much so that when they were all talking husbands she snapped a photo of it onto her phone.
After that it was a weekend for thinking. Freya knew that she had to tell Zack and she went by his office on the Monday morning but got cold feet.
'What I can do for you, Freya?' Zack said.
There were so many possible answers to that question that they even shared a smile, and Freya made up something about the Canadian hockey player. It served its purpose and diverted them back to work, and Zack got cross but it was clear the lust remained.
Freya was now swiping oolong tea every time she went past one of the waiting rooms just to keep hydrated as she was throwing up so often.
'How are you?' James stopped by her office.
Lately he seemed to be doing that a lot.
'I'm fine.'
'That doesn't mean anything with you,' James

said, and finally he told her what was on his mind. 'You've lost weight.'

'James...' Freya took a breath. 'Every time I drop a couple of pounds it doesn't have to mean that I'm back to sticking my fingers down my throat.'

'I didn't say that. I asked if you were okay.'

'Well, I am.'

'Good.'

'And while we're discussing the great white elephant of my eating disorder,' Freya said, 'I'm going to start taking clients. I'm having some cards made up. If you want me to see them elsewhere...'

'Are you sure you're not taking on too much?'

'Do I ever ask you that?'

'Actually, yes,' James said. 'I've got to go. I've got interviews but I'll let the others know that you're taking on clients and if they have anyone who might benefit from a referral.' He gave a roll of his eyes. 'That's half my patient list, actually. I don't think you'll ever need to advertise.' He turned at the sound of Zack's footsteps coming down the corridor. 'I'm just about to start interviewing for your replacement.'

'Not now,' Zack clipped. 'I've got a patient to see.'

He was dreading it.

It was the last-chance saloon for this little mite and his parents knew it.

All night he had been up late, speaking with colleagues, going over and over the ultrasounds with the best brains he knew, and the response had been the same. Zack would take on more than most, which was why his stats came in low, but in this…

Zack sat with the twenty-year-old mother and the twenty-two-year-old father and he told them as best as he could that their son would die.

'Please,' Rachael begged. 'Can you at least try…?'

And he went through it all over again, how the damage was too much and that his system was collapsing.

'He'd very likely die on the operating table, or shortly post-operatively,' Zack said. 'Or he can die in your arms.'

Zack could have gone then but he stayed and spoke with them extensively and made sure they understood he wasn't simply giving up on their son.

Sometimes you didn't get a choice.

Like ten years to this day when his brother had died.

It was not a good day at the office!

Freya tried not to notice Stephanie's raised eyebrows as she came out of one of the patients' very luxurious restrooms. She hadn't been able to make it to the staff one.

Oh, no. If Stephanie mentioned to James that she'd seen Freya dash off to vomit, he'd have her back in rehab by the end of the week.

And there was Zack, handing over his pagers.

'I'm not on call tonight,' Zack said to Stephanie.

'I'll call if there's anything urgent with one of your patients—'

'I said that I'm not on call tonight.' Zack made things clear to Stephanie. 'I'm going to get blind.'

'Oh.'

He was as grey as she'd seen him and they

didn't bother with small talk as they walked out to their cars.

'Freya...' he called her over as she climbed into her car.

'Yes?'

She turned and looked up at him and Zack stared back and he honestly didn't know what to say, he hadn't even meant to call out to her.

He needed her tonight.

Sex, yes, but he wanted all the rest tonight too. Hell, he'd even take the green smoothie.

Just because he didn't want to move in it didn't mean he had wanted it to end, and he was kicking himself for doing what he did best—put on his boots and get out.

'How have you been since Cleo?'

He didn't get to know that, Freya decided. 'It happens.' She went to walk off and then remembered what she'd heard. 'I heard that you lost a patient today. I'm sorry.'

'It happens,' Zack said, but it nearly killed him when it did, especially one so tiny.

Especially today.

And she looked at his eyes and he said not a

word of that but she knew him, and she could feel the want between them.

And that was why she cried each night. She was crazy about this guy.

'You've lost weight,' Zack said.

'Oh, here we go. Have you been talking to James?'

'No,' Zack said. 'Is he worried?'

'James is always worried.'

'Does he have reason to be?'

'No.'

'Freya, I know I didn't end things very well.'

'There was nothing to end, Zack. It was sex, we both agreed to that and no more, and as good as it was...'

Their eyes met at the memory and Zack looked very deep into her eyes. She could not believe his gall.

Yes, his eyes were asking her for that.

'You are kidding me,' Freya said. Did he really think they were going to have sex?

She wanted to so much.

To just ignore that she was completely incapable of *not* wanting a relationship with this man and to take the good they had.

It would be too much for her heart to bear, though. She had to tell him about the baby, but she could see his anguish today so Freya chose not to now. She abruptly pulled back from telling him and got angry instead.

"You know what, Zack? We should have kept it at one night. Life was so much easier when I didn't know your name.'

Freya climbed into her car and reversed out angrily.

She wanted him—oh, my, she wanted him.

But even if they had kept it at one night, she'd still be in trouble.

Freya drove towards home and hoped she wasn't too late to let Cleo out and then she remembered that Cleo wasn't there any more.

And so instead of knowing that patient black eyes awaited her, Freya had the joy of chatting with herself on the drive home.

She had to tell Zack.

Or not.

He'd be gone in a few weeks.

And she'd been considering donor eggs and donor sperm after all.

But the donors *chose* anonymity and it would be her baby's right to know, and Zack had the right to know too.

He'd find out anyway soon.

Stephanie was gossiping, Freya knew, and she trusted Zack wouldn't just assume her eating disorder was back.

They had both messed up that first night but it wasn't a disaster. Freya had it all under control.

She was thirty-one, she'd planned to be a single mom.

Zack deserved to know and he also deserved to know that she neither needed nor expected nothing from him.

Freya took the exit and then joined the traffic heading into the city.

She left her car with the valet and walked into the hotel and went straight to the elevators. Down a familiar corridor she walked, but with a different type of anticipation knotting her stomach now as she tried to guess his reaction.

There was a 'Do not disturb' sign on the door and Freya ignored it and knocked.

'Read the sign,' came his deep, surly voice in response to her knock on the door.

'Zack, it's...' Freya started, and then she had the appalling thought that he might be in there with someone he might have met in the elevator or bar and was banging his brains out, as was clearly his chosen stress response. But then the door opened and he had on only a towel, and then she glanced over his wet, naked shoulder and saw that, no, there was no one else in his suite.

'I'm just in the middle of a phone call,' Zack said.

'Do you want me to wait outside?' Freya offered.

'No, no,' he said, and as she walked into his suite he caught her off guard and pulled her in. 'Thank God,' Zack breathed into her ear, and then his mouth was on hers in a hungry kiss and she got a slab of wet muscle pressed into her. It took Freya a second to register that he had assumed she was taking him up on his earlier offer.

'Zack...'

'I won't be long,' Zack mouthed, and put his finger to his lips and then walked over to the bed and picked up the phone he had left there. 'Sorry, Mum, it was just the maid.'

He gave her a wink and took her right back to their first conversation and straight back to when all they had been was sex. Freya stood there, her dress damp from his freshly showered body, and she tasted him as she licked her lips. She was unsure what to do as Zack carried on the conversation and she could actually see the tension in his back as he tried to keep his patience as he spoke with his mum.

'Alice has a right to have a life…it's been ten years,' Zack said. 'She's allowed to go out on his anniversary. We don't have to sit behind the curtains to grieve.'

Oh, God, it was the anniversary of his brother's death, Freya realised as he spoke on.

On top of it all he was dealing with that today.

He went over and got out another glass and went to pour her some wine from an open bottle.

Freya shook her head and he held up some water and she nodded.

'Why don't we at least try it tomorrow?' Zack said. 'It's all set up and we can speak face to face wherever I am in the world.'

He gave Freya a smile that said, thank God he wasn't video chatting with his parents today, because the towel was lifting and Freya, who hadn't properly smiled in a long time, found that she was.

He put ice and lemon in her water and then, while dealing with this very difficult conversation, he came over and placed it down on the desk. And there was one little problem, Freya realised.

Well, there were many, many problems, but he thought she was there for sex and the sight of him naked and a taste of his tongue, and, as his hand slid around her waist, she was turned on.

Okay, sex tonight, and she'd tell him tomorrow, Freya thought, and she stood.

Or, should she just write 'I'M PREGNANT' on the little hotel pad now and pass him a note?

Zack was just finishing up the conversation as his fingers worked her breasts. Her thick nipples told him she was just on the edge of getting her period and he loved the intensity of a woman's orgasm then.

He turned off the phone and was just so relieved that call was over and especially that she was here and his response told her so.

This kiss was as fierce as their first. It was actually more so because it toppled her back onto the bed.

'Freya.' He said it like a moan. He was kissing her face, her mouth, her ears and just pressing her into the bed. Her legs were over the edge and he was roughly parting them and just tearing at her knickers but Freya was hungrily kissing him back.

She was holding his face just to keep it still enough for her mouth and then she gave in and held onto his shoulders as Zack seared inside.

His feet were on the floor and his elbows were each side of her head.

He thrust in hard and the friction they generated meant neither would last. Her legs wrapped around him as all the hurts of past weeks were gathered into an intense peak.

Freya came, a beat before he did, and it was

a come so deep that it demanded him now and Zack spilled into her.

'God, but I needed you tonight.' He really did, so much so that he had been planning to head to Freya's because living like this wasn't working. 'What made you change your mind and come over?'

He saw her rapid blink.

'Freya?'

'I came here to talk to you…'

'What?'

He replayed the events and Zack pulled out and got up and whipped a towel around his hips and looked at her as she pulled down her dress.

'I didn't force you?'

'Zack,' Freya said, 'I might not have come with the intention of sex but I was a very willing participant.'

'But you came here to talk?'

'Yes.'

He was still going over it in his head. 'For a moment there I thought…'

'Thought what?'

'It doesn't matter,' Zack said. 'What did you want to talk about?'

'I'm pregnant.' It came out faster than she'd intended.

It just came out.

He hadn't had even a hint that she was and there was no lead in, no warning, she just hit him right with it.

'You choose your moments, don't you?' Zack said.

'I thought I'd tell you when you weren't working…'

'I lost a six-week-old today, I've got my parents on the phone, crying about St Toby and all the grandchildren they haven't got. Should I ring them back and tell them I'm going to be a father?' He went on, 'But do you know what, Freya? I wouldn't do that to them on a day like today!'

'I didn't know it was the anniversary of your brother,' Freya said. 'We don't know enough about each other to do specific dates.'

'I lost a six-week-old today!' Zack said. 'How's that for a specific day because his parents will remember it for ever!'

'Zack?'

'You know for a moment there, I thought...'

'What?'

He shook his head. He had honestly, for a moment there, thought that Freya had got him.

That the woman he had first met had come to his room and that they were back to the beginning but with history and understanding now.

That maybe, just maybe he'd met someone who things might work out with, but he had only just been starting to think like that and now Freya had her voice on.

'Now, I know it's a lot to take in, Zack, but—'

'Don't do your psychologist voice with me,' he warned. 'Don't tell me it's a major life-changing event, but that soon I'll—'

'It doesn't have to mean a major life change.'

He looked at her.

'Er...do I have a say here?' Zack checked, but there was still a warning note to his voice. Was she popping by to tell him she was on her way to get a termination?

'That's why I'm here, Zack.'

'Stop calling me Zack in that voice,' he hissed.

Freya was using her patient and reasonable and very together voice and it was driving him insane.

'I'm not having a termination.'

Zack looked at her as she told him how things would be, as Freya, because it was Freya, dealt with all the current things on her to-do list.

'I was already looking into fertility treatments and donors—'

'Oh, so I've done my job, then.'

'You're being petulant.'

'I feel petulant,' Zack said.

'I'm just saying that I've thought this through and there's no need for you to get worked up. I can more than cope with single motherhood.'

'That's good to know,' Zack said, but with an edge. 'And do I get to see my child in this plan you've made?'

'If you choose to, then I'm sure we can sort that out.'

'You've really thought this through.'

'I have,' Freya said. 'So when I have your thoughts we can make plans or not.'

'Are you worried, upset?' Zack checked. 'You were just getting back into psychology.'

'I don't see that one has to exclude the other.'

'Are you—?'

'Zack, I'm thirty-one,' Freya interrupted his questions. 'I was already planning on single parenthood. I'm not going to fall in a heap.'

'You don't like it when the tables are turned, do you?' Zack said. 'You want my thoughts, yet you refuse to give yours.'

'Ask away,' Freya said.

'Okay, what about us?'

'You've made it clear that it's just sex you want from me.' Freya put her nose in the air as if she disapproved.

'You don't want sex?' Zack asked, and she didn't answer. 'Well,' he said.

Freya pressed her lips together. She didn't know this mood. He was arrogant and angry yet there was this twist of a smile on his face that she didn't get.

Zack carried on. 'With all this sexual attraction do Mommy and Daddy do it when you drop the baby off?'

'I don't know where this is leading, Zack.'

Oh, my God, Zack thought, she'd just used that voice again.

'Well, you've been so busy sorting it out I just wondered if that was covered already. Curious...' Freya could see that black smile was there and it wasn't the news he seemed annoyed with but her.

Freya.

The woman, Freya knew, that he didn't want to have a relationship with.

'What about the two of us?'

'No,' Freya said. 'I lived through my parents' unhappy marriage. I'm not inflicting it on my child.'

'You jump straight to marriage.' His grin was incredulous now!

'I'm saying that I don't want a marriage, I want to do this on my own. Of course you'll be entitled to access.'

'Do you know what I like about you, Freya?' Zack said. 'You've got it all worked out.'

Freya looked at him.

'Do you know what I don't like about you,

Freya? That you've got it all worked out without me.'

'I don't understand.'

'That's okay.' Zack shrugged. 'I'm not in the mood for explaining. Well, thank you for dropping by.'

He stood and went to the door.

'Are you asking me to leave?'

'Yes.' Zack said. 'Pay attention to the sign next time. If it says don't disturb, don't disturb.'

'But we need to talk.'

'We already have.'

'I need your thoughts.'

'Well, you can't have them yet.'

He didn't have a clue what they were.

CHAPTER SIXTEEN

His HANGOVER WAS impressive and instead of going to The Hills, where no doubt Freya would be tapping her feet, waiting for him to snap to her snappy tune, he took the morning off and in the afternoon he drove into South LA and to the Bright Hope Clinic.

'Mila's not here today,' Geoff said.

'I know. I'm just dropping by to see how things are going.'

'Well, we're taking delivery of an MRI machine tomorrow,' Geoff told him, 'and I've just ordered a state-of-the-art ultrasound that might mean we can have intelligent conversations...'

It had been frustrating. Knowing that The Hill's equipment would give clearer answers, there had been a lot of doubling up. Zack wanted state of the art, so nearly every test Geoff had done had been repeated.

'It's great news about Paulo.'

'I think he'll be going home soon,' Zack said.

They went through the patients and Geoff said he'd like to come and watch the scheduled ablation.

'On a Sunday?' Zack checked. 'And it's Valentine's Day.'

'My wife is very understanding.'

Zack saw a few patients and then drove back to the hotel and lay on the bed with his hands behind his head and tried to make some sense of his thoughts.

He took out his laptop and typed in a few things, and found out that their baby, assuming it had been conceived on the first night, was due on September twenty-fourth.

He stared at that date for ages and then he texted Freya.

Are you okay?

She took less than a minute to respond.

I've told you I'm fine with it.

He fired back another text.

Such a well thought-out response!

Then he deleted it, unsent, and wrote another.

Let me know if you need anything.

She wouldn't.

That much Zack knew.

He still couldn't get over how she'd been the night Cleo had died. Even he had teared up but not Freya. It was like she kept all her emotions inside and yet he had glimpsed them.

The things she'd told him, Zack knew, only he knew.

And it worked both ways. Freya knew stuff he would never discuss with anyone else.

She had pushed too hard and too soon, though, Zack thought, but then he smiled as he did so because that was Freya.

They were so good together and she had wanted more, and he could see now that she'd probably known she was pregnant and starting to stress.

His head was a mess and there was no one he

could talk to, or was it that there was no one he would talk to?

His alarm went off and Zack remembered that his mother had reluctantly agreed to try video-chatting.

Zack sat up and picked up the laptop.

This should be fun!

Not.

After a few goes, there was his mum and she had make-up on, when she only wore it at Christmas or on birthdays.

'How are you?' Zack smiled when he saw her.

'Sorry about yesterday.'

It had been a very tense phone call, which was why Zack could not have been more relieved when Freya had arrived.

'It's fine,' Zack said. 'Yesterday was a tough one.'

'You're right,' Judy said. 'Alice deserves to be happy.'

'So do you guys,' Zack said. 'Where's Dad?'

'He's in with a patient. Max is here for a check-up.'

'How is he doing?'

'Very well,' Judy said. 'I was thinking when you come home in April...'

And that was the trouble with communicating like this. Judy saw Zack close his eyes.

'You've changed your mind?'

'No,' Zack said, but how did he tell his mother that things here in LA had suddenly got very complicated? They didn't speak about such things.

Could they?

'I've got some stuff going on at the moment...'

'Another patient who needs you?'

'Isn't Dad the same?' Zack challenged, and Judy smiled.

'I guess.'

'Anyway, it isn't work that's complicated,' Zack said. 'I like someone.'

His mother said nothing.

'A lot.'

'You can tell me, Zack.'

'I'm trying to.'

'Times are changing.' Judy sat very composed and Zack looked at her, and then his face went right up to the screen.

'Do you think I'm gay?'

He could not believe it.

'You've never had a lady friend,' Judy said. 'Tara had a thing for you and you never did anything about it…'

He'd been trying to keep Tara's dad from knowing! 'Mum, just because I don't discuss my sex life with you it doesn't mean that I don't have one.'

'I'm talking about relationships. You've never spoken about anyone special and I was worried that you felt you couldn't tell me.'

'There hasn't really been anyone special,' Zack said. 'Till now.'

'And you said that there would never be grandchildren.'

'Because I could never see myself as a parent or tied down.' And he sat there in silence, with his mum doing the same, and it wasn't a strained silence this time. He didn't feel tied down with Freya. That morning when she'd suggested he move in had jolted the hell out of him but he could laugh about that now. That was Freya. It was who she was.

'I need to work a few things out,' he said.

'Well, I think that's a very good reason not to come home,' Judy said. 'Does *she* have a name?'

He was about to say 'Fred' but realised his mum maybe wouldn't get his joke. 'Freya.'

And he named her.

He named the woman who, wherever they were headed, was in his life.

Freya and Zack.

'I might have a glass of sherry tonight,' Judy said, and Zack laughed.

'I am coming home soon,' he told her, and he thought about what Freya had said. 'Maybe for two or three months. I could help out properly and give you and Dad a break.'

'That would be wonderful.' Judy smiled. 'But sort yourself out first and while you're at it, get a haircut.'

And the relationship that had always been difficult was being worked on and it felt good that it was.

'There's your dad. I'll let him say bye to Tara and then go and fetch him.'

'Can I see Max?'

He wanted to see the little guy.

 After a little bit of drama getting them all on the sofa and the computer in place, there was Tara and they shared a smile.

'Thank you,' Tara said.

He looked at his ex and the feelings were only of friendship, both knew that, but all these years on and, without talking, this friendship remained a good one.

It wouldn't have.

Both knew that had they stayed together and made promises that the other could not keep, they would have been fighting and, yep, a divorce statistic now. And he thought of Toby and Alice. It had been such a hard secret to carry but Freya knew it now and that helped.

'This is Max,' Tara said. 'The cause of all this drama.'

'He looks fantastic. Cale told me that the surgery went really well.'

'It did,' Tara said. 'But apparently we got there just in time. He collapsed in the air ambulance.'

Jed, Tara's husband, spoke then. 'We're very

grateful to the surgeon and to you and Dr Carlton. You made a great team.'

Even if they'd only managed to work as a team that once, it was a great result. Max was healthy and starting to cry and Tara tried to quiet him with her finger as Jed spoke on. 'I was saying to Tara it's hard to imagine now but in a few years he'll be bringing in the cows...'

And Zack looked at a very little infant that would probably be as strapping as his father one day and there were all the assumptions there, but then Tara spoke.

'Max gets a chance to be anything he wants to be now.'

It was a little message between her and Zack.

'He does,' Zack agreed.

'Thanks, Zack.' Tara smiled. 'You'll be sure to stop by when you're home?'

'I shall.'

They stood and walked off and left Zack with his dad. No doubt his mum was leading them through to the kitchen where she would have some cake ready. It was never just a visit for some patients.

Zack could remember most days getting in from school and the lounge would be full with patients, or families of patients.

'I've been tough on you, Zack,' his father said.

'And I get why you have been,' Zack said. 'I hate that it all falls down to you. And I do worry about you retiring and what's going to happen but—'

'You've got your life.' His father said it without malice now.

'I'm good at what I do,' Zack said. 'I need to stick with it. In the same way you stuck with general practice when it was tempting to go to the city.'

He was about to tell his dad his plans to come back, maybe at Christmas so that he and his mother could have a break, maybe take a holiday, but then Zack smiled to himself. If things worked out, and he hoped that they would, there was no way his parents would be heading off on a holiday the next time their son came home.

Whatever happened between him and Freya there would, God willing, be a grandchild for them to get to know.

Now he just had to sort things out with the person who thought she had it all sorted out—Miss Freya.

CHAPTER SEVENTEEN

HE WAS OVER at Bright Hope the next day and made no effort to contact her. His lack of response to the issue drove Freya insane.

And then, when he finally did rock up at The Hills, at ten the next day, he gave absolutely no indication as to his thoughts or feelings.

He kept her on the boil all week and she made an excuse to have to be there on Saturday afternoon, just because she knew he was passing through.

Zack had brought cake.

A great big white chocolate cake piled with fresh raspberries and the staff all oohed and ahhed and Freya sat there in the staffroom, trying to fathom its meaning.

For a clue.

And she was still searching for the secret sign

when he came down and sat opposite her, having cut a large slice. He crossed his long legs and gave her a smile.

'How are you, Freya?'

'I'm very well, thank you.'

'I don't usually see you here at the weekends.'

'I've got a consulting room for my future clients that I'm setting up,' Freya said, which was true, but she was hardly grappling with an Allen key. This was The Hills after all. Her consulting room was gorgeous. It was attached to her office and Freya had chosen the artwork and rugs to ensure that it was an oasis of calm.

'Did James mention that I might have a client for you?' Zack checked, and Freya shook her head.

'I haven't seen James today.'

'Her name's Emily, she's nineteen years old. I'm seeing her sister. Her mother mentioned some of the issues that she was having with her daughter. I gave her your card to give to Emily if the time was right.'

'Thank you.'

Stephanie stood up. 'Thanks for the cake, Zack, it was a lovely gesture.'

'No problem.'

She walked off and Freya sat there facing him.

'Cake?' Freya asked.

'Do you want some?' Zack pretended that he didn't know what she meant.

'No!' She wanted to know what the hell he was thinking. The only change in him she could see was that he'd brought in a cake and was sitting there with almost a smile on his face.

'Why cake?'

'Because I was pretty off the other day, with Stephanie and a couple of others, when the baby died, and I thought I'd apologise to the staff.' He stood. 'It's not all about you, Freya.'

'We need to talk.'

'When I'm ready,' Zack said. 'Anyway, what's the rush? You've already got it all worked out.'

She closed her eyes in frustration.

'And we've got months to sort things out,' Zack reminded her, and Freya shushed him.

'I want this sorted. I want to know what your plans are.'

'When I've decided I'll be sure to let you know.'

'You're the most annoying—'

'Why?' Zack said. 'I only jump into bed, Freya, not to your tune, and *my* thoughts are measured.'

'Meaning?'

'Just that,' Zack said. 'No deeper meaning. Do you want to go out for dinner tonight?'

She stared at him and she hated that, yes, she tried to search for a deeper meaning to his offer.

'Yes.'

'I'll pick you up at six.'

'Six?' Freya said. 'Are we going to check out the children's menu for future reference?'

He resisted laughing. 'I'm operating early tomorrow, I need to be in bed at a reasonable hour.'

And he still had that smile and she was still, still searching for deeper meaning in every word he said.

He set her on fire.

Just that.

She was squirming on the inside and wondering if it was dinner and bed together, or bed alone, if it was talking or what the hell went on in that beautiful head.

He gave her no clue.

Zack cut himself another slice of cake and walked out.

CHAPTER EIGHTEEN

'Hɪ...'

Freya had just put the final touches to the consulting room and was about to dash home for a quick shower and change before her very early dinner with Zack when the phone in her office rang.

She was about to let it go to the machine but at the last minute changed her mind and was very glad she had when she heard the nervous young voice.

'My name's Emily...' the young woman said, and then she started to cry. 'I've just done it again.'

'It's okay,' Freya said. Whatever Emily had done, it wasn't the point right now, but that she'd called was so, so important that Freya wasn't going to waste time questioning her for details.

'It's okay,' Freya said, and gradually the sobbing stopped.

Freya just listened as Emily told her that she'd had a massive binge and purge and her mother, who was already worried sick about her sister, had found her and was now upstairs, crying.

'She doesn't need this,' Emily sobbed.

And Freya thought of James, who had tried so hard to be a parent for her, and the anguish she had caused him, and how relieved he'd been when she had accepted help.

'Are you going to tell her that you've called me?'

'Yes.'

'Well, I think she'll be very relieved to know that you're talking to someone about it. So that might be something you can tell her when we've finished chatting.' They spoke for a few moments until Emily had calmed down. 'Why don't you go to bed now?' Freya said, knowing how drained Emily would be. 'Tell your mom that you're coming in to see me tomorrow at nine. Would that be okay?'

'It's a Sunday.'

'That's okay,' Freya said.

They spoke a little more, but Emily really was exhausted and Freya was glad that her plan for her to tell her mom and meet tomorrow seemed to have given her some measure of relief.

'I'll see you in the morning, Emily,' Freya said, and then the oddest smile came to her lips as she realised Zack was right and she had her *voice,* as he called it, on. 'I'm looking forward to meeting you,' Freya said, more normally. 'Go and speak to your mom and then get some rest.'

Of course Freya did some major overthinking on the drive to her apartment, wondering if she should have seen Emily straight away, but there was no real point speaking at length with Emily tonight.

And she wasn't going to be available every time her clients had a binge.

Emily needed to rest and recover and get some fluid into her...

Tomorrow.

They would start this journey tomorrow. She just hoped that Emily didn't cancel, because that first reaching out was the hardest, Freya knew.

She had fifteen minutes to get ready when she had hoped to have thirty and Freya quickly peeled off her clothes as she turned on the shower, and then everything stopped.

There was a flash of blood in her knickers and when she saw it, Freya was convinced she was losing her baby.

Everything in her world just stopped and the panic that hit had her frantic. She felt like a cat with its tail on fire and yet she was crouched, kneeling on the bathroom floor, and, she was sure, losing her baby.

'No...'

And it was all her fault, for not eating, for running, for riding and for believing for a second that she could be a mother. She felt as if she was back to being seventeen and being told her bones would one day crumble and she'd never be able to have babies. Freya was sobbing so violently she couldn't breathe.

She could hear someone knocking at the door and then they started to knock louder.

Realising that it must be Zack, Freya pulled a towel from the rail and, barely covered, wrenched open the door. Zack saw her red face and angry eyes and this time there *were* tears streaming down, and because she was scared she hit out with words.

'Panic over!'

She never cried, never, ever, but they were pouring out now. 'I've lost it,' she shouted to him, 'so panic over.'

'Freya…' He was so calm that it angered her further. 'I'm not panicking.'

'Because you don't care!' she screamed. 'You didn't want it anyway.'

'Tell me what's happened.' His voice was normal and it made hers sound all the more mad. 'Are you bleeding?'

She was holding up a towel and Zack looked down at her legs and there was no blood that he could see.

'Yes, I'm bleeding!'

'Come on.' He led her to the bedroom.

'I knew I'd never be able to have children, after all I've done to myself, I don't deserve them, you don't want them…'

And he remembered her 'I shot my ovaries'

comment and knew that all the loathing was aimed at herself.

'How much are you bleeding?'

He was still so completely calm, like a doctor, only he wasn't the doctor, he was the father, and she hit out at him but he caught her wrist.

'Freya.'

She'd lost her towel on the way to the bedroom and Zack sat her on the bed. 'How much bleeding is there?'

He looked at her and she seemed fine and he heard the shower and went in and the relief that hit when he saw the tiny amount in her knickers was something he kept to himself.

She was a mess.

He looked out towards the bedroom where Freya was sobbing and curled up in a ball on the bed. Whatever he had intended to say over dinner would just have to wait now. He turned off the taps in the shower and went back into the bedroom.

'Have you got any cramping?'

'No.'

'Everything might well be fine...'

She couldn't believe it.

He tried to unfold her tight body but she wouldn't relax and he got onto the bed beside her and brought her cold body against his warm one. 'Match my breathing,' he said. It was like he was breathing for her, and she tried to get hers as slow and as deep, and then he spoke.

'Freya, a lot of women get bleeding. You're eight weeks pregnant—'

'Six.'

'Eight,' he corrected her, and smiled because sometimes he forgot she had studied brains, not bodies. 'You add two weeks.'

How was he smiling and talking, all calm and normally? It wasn't because he didn't care, she knew that because he was lying on the bed beside her and she was curled into him.

'Did you lose anything in the shower?'

'I didn't get into the shower,' Freya said. 'I just saw the blood and I freaked...'

'I know,' Zack said. 'Well, I don't exactly.'

How was she, Freya wondered, breathing and calming and starting to believe that it might be okay? And then she remembered how she had lashed out before. She had utterly lost it and it was something she had fought all her life not to do.

'Turn over,' Zack said.

'I can't,' Freya admitted. She had screamed, she had hit at him, she had shown her worst self and all her fears, so how could she turn around?

'We can go now and do an ultrasound,' Zack said.

'No.' Freya shook her head. 'I don't want anyone at The Hills knowing.'

'They won't. I can—'

'No.'

'Have you got an OB?'

Freya nodded. 'I'm seeing someone for fertility so I already had an appointment for next week.'

'Do you want to call her and see if I can drive you in?'

'On a Saturday night?'

'Yes,' Zack said, and then he realised she might be stalling. 'Do you want to see someone?'

'I don't want to find out,' Freya said. 'I just want one more night where I might be pregnant. I don't want to know yet if I've lost it. Zack, I've wanted a baby for years, I honestly thought I couldn't have one. I wasn't using you.'

'I know that.' Zack said. 'Who told you that you couldn't have children?'

'In rehab,' Freya said. 'I had stopped menstruating and they said I was a shoe-in for infertility, osteoporosis…'

'Whoever said what they did was trying to scare you into eating.' He could only guess the damage of knowing for years that you'd blown your chances. 'They were clearly talking rubbish.'

She turned around in his arms and he gave her such a nice smile.

'Do you really think that I might still be pregnant?'

'Well, I haven't been anywhere near that field for many years but, yes, a little show, no cramping. I think it happens a lot.'

And from hell she entered calmer waters.

'I'm sorry you saw me like that.'

'I'm very glad that I saw you like that,' Zack said, and Freya closed her eyes.

She knew she'd blown any chance for them now.

They lay for a while, Freya becoming calmer, Zack thinking.

'You've got surgery tomorrow,' Freya said, remembering he'd said he needed an early night.

'I do.' Zack nodded. 'I'll go and make something to eat.'

Zack got out of bed and went into the kitchen. He bypassed all the little measuring cups and returned to the room with two bowls of lovely creamy pasta.

'We'll go and get you checked tomorrow. I'll call work and have them reschedule.'

'No.' Freya shook her head. It was his Sunday list and there were so many people relying on him. 'Unless things get worse, you ought to go in. I've got to go in as well—I've got that young girl coming in. It would be awful for her if I cancelled.'

'Okay.'

His calm control seeped into her.

They ate pasta and she found out he could cook and they lay in bed and watched a movie. Zack noticed something on the bedside table and asked what it was.

'Cleo's ashes.'

'No way!' Zack said, and he wasn't Mr Nice now. He took them straight out to the lounge room. 'I can't sleep with them next to me.'

'Are you staying?'

'Freya?' Zack checked. 'You really think I'd leave you now?'

'You want an early night.'

'And you need one!'

He got into bed.

'You're not keeping the ashes, are you?'

'I don't know.' She looked at him. 'Are they freaking you?'

'A bit.'

'I didn't think anything freaked you.'

'I'm a mystery,' Zack said.

He turned out the light and he was back in her bed when she had never thought he would be.

'I really am a mystery,' Zack said. 'It turns out that my mother thought I was gay.'

Freya laughed and she told him about the hotel events coordinator checking him out when he'd checked in.

It was nice to lie in the dark, talking and then falling quiet.

'So, is this what parenthood looks like?' Zack said when she was feeling a little calmer. 'Knot in your chest and no sex?'

'I think so.'

He rolled over and put his hand on her stomach and then he said the nicest thing.

'I want you to be pregnant,' he said. 'I want the baby.'

And, because it was Zack, she knew he meant it.

'So hang in there, little one.'

CHAPTER NINETEEN

ZACK WOKE TO the mechanical sound of a blender.

Get used to it, Zack, he told himself, because he might well be waking to it for the rest of his life.

And so, as Freya pulped broccoli and blueberries and did what she had to do to keep her place on this planet in order, she watched as a dishevelled, barely dressed, sexy Australian came out of the bedroom and walked out of her apartment.

And there was no feeling of dread when he left this time.

A few moments later he walked back in with a tin of coffee, which kept his part of the planet in better order, and they shared a smile.

'Why do you have coffee in your car?' Freya asked.

'Because I like coffee in the morning and I know you don't have any.'

'Oh, so were you intending on staying last night.'

'Yep,' Zack said. 'Well, I was hoping to.'

And she opened a cupboard and showed him that she had indeed bought some coffee since he'd walked out.

He wrapped his arms around her and Freya let herself be wrapped in them.

'Any bleeding?' he asked.

'None.'

'How do you feel?'

'Better,' Freya said.

She couldn't give a completely honest answer— that the world felt safer just for the fact that he was next to her now. Freya knew she pushed too hard, pressed for too much, and so she held it back.

Last night he had taken such precious care of her and she let herself be grateful for that.

And so, getting into separate cars, they both waved to Red and then headed into work.

Today would be a day that Freya found out how strong she was. Maybe pregnant, maybe not, and with her love life in shreds because Zack was probably thinking what hell was he going to have to co-parent with after her outburst last night.

And yet she could put it aside.

Not too far aside, because her issues came with her, and they were needed today.

For a long time Freya had doubted if she was the right person for this role, whether she had healed herself enough to offer advice to someone going through what once she had.

Now, though, she knew it was a lifelong journey and she had learned so much on this path.

'Thank you for seeing me,' Emily said.

They sat in her new consulting room and Freya told Emily she was her first client and then she told her a bit about herself. Emily said nothing at first, but when Freya mentioned her food diaries Emily got out her phone and Freya looked through it.

It was like looking back on her own life.

The exercise, the obsessions with food, the waiting till someone left the room so you could do a hundred more sit-ups. The agony of a cruel disease. Emily wasn't dangerously thin but, Freya knew, the real battle was in her mind.

They went way over time and Emily laughed at the end when Freya said, 'You're far more honest than I was.'

'There's no point lying any more,' Emily said. 'I just want to get well.'

Emily would do well, Freya was sure.

They made another appointment for Thursday.

'Just to let you know,' Freya said, 'that I might be having a small procedure during the week, so if I have to reschedule, that's why.'

'I'm sorry to have messed up your Sunday.'

'You didn't,' Freya answered. 'It's good to get things under way.'

Emily left and Freya knew that she felt better and so too did she. It had been right to come in today and it was time to get something else under way. Freya was ready to know now if she was pregnant or not so she called Hilary.

'Hi, Freya.'

'Sorry to call on a Sunday,' Freya said.

'I doubt you would without reason,' Hilary said. 'What's happening?'

'I got a positive pregnancy test, I think I'm eight weeks,' Freya said, 'but then last night I bled.'

'Are you still bleeding?'

'No.'

'Any pain?'

'No.'

And Hilary asked some more questions just as calmly as Zack had. 'Do you want to come in today?' she offered.

'On a Sunday?'

'Babies keep their own schedules,' Hilary said. 'I tend to write off uninterrupted weekends, that's why my vacations are taken overseas.'

As Freya walked out she stopped at James's office. He was a complete workaholic and catching up on some files.

'Hi,' Freya said.

'Freya.' He gave her a nod. 'How was your first client?'

'It went well,' Freya said. 'It was helpful to me too. Thank you, James, for all you did for me back then.'

'I'm your brother,' James said. 'Freya, are you okay?'

'I am,' Freya said.

She was.

However it all unfolded, Freya knew now she would be okay.

'Are we talking?' Freya checked.

'Not really,' James said.

But he was still her brother.

He gave her a smile and Freya headed off, alone, to find out about the baby.

She loved Zack and however he felt about her, or them, she could handle it. That he wanted the baby meant the world. If they got the chance to be, they would be good parents. Possibly unconventional ones, with a father who drifted, but when he was there, Freya knew that he'd be the best dad in the world.

Freya sat in her car for a moment before going in and when tears came she shed them.

She just let them happen for the first time as she acknowledged she wanted *this* baby so much.

This father.

This miracle.

This life and this world.

And so in she went.

Hilary didn't care a jot about Freya's leaking eyes, she was more than used to them.

And then, just as Freya thought she had everything a little more under control, the most appalling thing happened, and she found out she *really* had no control.

'I feel sick,' Freya admitted, as her green breakfast rose in her stomach, and her eyes scanned the room for an exit, because, in her head, no one could see her do that.

'Are you going to throw up?' Hilary asked.

Absolutely she was.

In front of another person!

And there was no chance of being tidy and hidden any more.

'Feel better now?' Hilary asked a few minutes later as she calmly took away the little dish she kept for these moments.

Freya did.

She had cried, she had thrown up, she'd had a cuddle from Zack and had seen her first client, and she was being open and honest and vulnerable.

It was the oddest of days, the scariest of days, but it felt like the nicest too.

'I'm nervous to find out.'

'I know,' Hilary said.. 'Have you had a lot of vomiting?'

'Loads,' Freya said. 'And I got dizzy after my run. Should I have run?'

'Do you run regularly?'

'Yes.'

'Then that's fine. Just keep hydrated. You know your body.'

'Sex?' Freya asked.

'Well, that's how babies get there in the first place!'

They talked. Hilary knew already about Freya's past medical history and after answering some of Freya's questions Hilary had a few of her own.

'I admit that I'm confused. I'm looking at your notes and we were talking sperm and egg donors the last time I saw you.'

That seemed like such a long time ago.

'Do you know who the father is?' Hilary asked, and Freya laughed at the directness of the question.

'I nearly didn't,' she admitted. 'It was supposed to be no-name sex.'

'Ha-ha.'

Oh, and the world was so much better when you were honest.

'He's amazing,' Freya admitted.

'Does he know about the pregnancy?'

'Yes,' Freya said. 'He knows and we both want the baby. It's just a bit too soon to know if we want the other...' Then she looked at Hilary and a doctor's office doubled as a very nice confessional. 'Well, it's not too soon for me to know but I'm trying not to push and crowd him and just see where we go...'

And it was time to see where this pregnancy was going.

She lay on an examination table and Hilary had a feel of her flat stomach and squirted some jelly onto it.

'I guess you might not see much,' Freya said, 'given it's so early and...' She chatted to keep herself busy. 'I haven't got a full bladder, so you probably can't—'

'Freya,' Hilary asked, 'how often do you menstruate?'

'Every six months or so.'

'Okay.'

And she was going to be told, no, Freya knew, that maybe in six months or so's time that she could try again.

'Well, when your ovaries zap, they really zap,' Hilary said, and she turned the screen. 'What do you see?'

A map of the moon, Freya thought, and then she looked again and there was a tiny person, a little bean with a head and a flicker that was a heart.

'Oh...' Freya said, because she was still pregnant.

'And over here,' Hilary said, and Freya's eyes wandered to another little bean and another tiny flicker that was a heart.

'Beautiful embryos,' Hilary said. 'Their position is perfect and their heartbeats are strong and a very good rate...'

'Their?' Freya checked.

'Twins,' Hilary said. 'So get used to throwing up for a few more weeks. Double everything, including the fun.'

'What about the bleeding?'

'It happens,' Hilary said.

'Do I have to be careful?'

'I tend to find they stay put or not whatever a woman does,' Hilary said, 'and these two look to me like they're staying put.'

It was overwhelming, completely, and then she thought about telling Zack that they were having twins and she blew out a breath.

Oh!

Drifter Zack the father of twins.

Freya had blood taken and then thanked Hilary and walked out to her car. She sat there for ages and then drove home and collected Cleo's ashes, feeling so glad she'd told her about the baby before she had died.

Babies!

'Thank you,' Freya said, as she scattered her friend's ashes into the huge ocean that separated the US and Australia. It was a place Cleo had loved in younger days and she was so glad of the gift James had given her at a time she had been so fragile.

Not any more.

Oh, it was a sad and happy day and she watched the sun go down and thought of Cleo.

Her phone rang and when she saw it was Zack she answered it.

'Hi,' Freya said.

'You've been crying?'

'Yes, I scattered Cleo's ashes. And don't you dare suggest I get another dog.'

'How was your client?'

'It went well,' Freya said. 'How was surgery?'

'Long,' Zack said. 'Have you had any more bleeding?'

'No.'

'That's good.'

'It is,' Freya said. She didn't want to tell him the news over the phone and decided she'd wait till a more suitable time than the last time she'd dropped a bombshell on him.

'Freya, can I ask a favour? I'm going to be here all night and I'm supposed to be speaking to my parents. They're driving me mad with video chats. Can you stop by the hotel and bring my adaptor?'

'Adaptor?'

'I don't have US appliances and I need to charge my laptop.'

'Oh.'

Well, what chance did they have? Freya thought as she let herself into his hotel room. Even their plugs were wired differently.

Freya lay on the bed in a room that had seen an awful lot of their goings-on and she smiled and decided to pinch a shirt of Zack's while she was there.

And if he found out, so what?

It wasn't a crime to be in lust, she would tell him, and just leave the love part out.

She drove to The Hills and there was Stephanie and her beady eyes at Reception, mentally weighing Freya as she walked in.

'Hi, Freya.'

'Hi.' Freya smiled but didn't stop for conversation. Thanks to Stephanie, rumours were flying but because of her past everyone was assuming her eating disorder was back with a vengeance, rather than that she had a baby on board.

Two babies.

Yikes!

She knocked on his office door and waited.

'Come in,' Zack called, and as she stepped in

it dawned on Freya the possible real reason she was here.

The room was in darkness and, as memory served, Zack liked to unwind after Theatre.

'Did you get me here to give you…?' And then she stopped because there was a table and two places laid and it was lit by a candle.

'Valentine's Day,' Zack said.

Oh, so it was.

'What did you get me?' Zack asked.

'You don't do Valentine's Day,' Freya said. She had truly forgotten. 'Actually, I've never done Valentine's Day either.'

She sat at the table and as lovely as it all was it was dark.

'I can't see you,' Freya said, and he laughed and put the lights on.

'Better?' Zack said, and now that she could see him it was. 'I got you a present.'

'Are you trying to make me feel extra-awkward for forgetting?'

'I am.' Zack nodded.

'And then I'd have been accused of being over the top,' Freya said.

'You are over the top, Freya,' Zack said, and he went behind his desk and very carefully carried over a very large box.

Oh, no, Freya thought as he gingerly put it down, and she watched for movement and saw all the little holes punched in the box so it could breathe.

He'd got her a puppy.

And she didn't want one.

'Zack…'

'Just open it.'

'I don't want it.'

'You might when you see it.'

Twins and a dog, Freya thought. Well, there goes any chance of freedom for the next two decades. And what about dog jealousy? And yet of course she was going to love her new puppy, it had come from Zack after all and it beat stealing a shirt from his wardrobe.

Freya pulled back the lid, waiting for a wet nose to peek out, but it didn't.

The box was empty, except for one thing.

A ring.

'Where's my puppy?' Freya croaked.

'A puppy is a big commitment and you have to be very sure,' Zack said. 'Pretty much the same with this. Freya, marry me.'

'Oh, Zack.' Freya shook her head. 'It's way too soon...'

'Not for me.'

'You're marrying me because I'm pregnant.'

'Freya! One, we don't even know if you're pregnant. Two, I don't marry women because they're pregnant. In fact, usually I'd be running out of the door the same way you did the morning after we met.'

'Really?'

'I'd have had morning sickness just at the thought,' Zack said, 'but I don't feel like that with you. I am in love with you. You're the most difficult, grating person I have ever had the fortune to get to know, and I want to get to know more of you, every day.'

He gave her a smile, a self-satisfied one. 'You'll never be able to top that,' Zack said. 'Even with all your PR skills, you have to concede that I have organised the best Valentine's Day and you, Freya, didn't even get me a card.'

'Of course I did,' Freya said, and she went into her bag and handed him a card, well, a photo of her ultrasound.

'Top that,' Freya said, and she watched his mouth open as he realised that, yes, Freya was pregnant and, because he could read ultrasounds far more easily than Freya, he saw straight away that it was twins.

He laughed.

He had everything he'd dreaded having for so long, but everything had changed—he wanted it all now. With Her.

They had arms and legs and heads and they were so much more than hers or his, they were theirs.

Then Freya watched as his laughter died and tears pooled in his complex eyes.

He wanted his brother to have had this moment.

Zack wanted his brother to this day and for ever he would.

'If we have a boy, can we call him Toby?'

'Yes.'

'He was so unhappy...'

'Not all of him was unhappy and he had someone he could speak to,' Freya said. 'His last night was spent under the stars, drinking and being honest with you. That's a very nice last night to have had on this earth. I know that I'd take it.'

She turned his world around.

The last night of his brother's life had always been an agonising memory.

Not now.

Zack could now, without reservations, remember their laughter and two brothers talking and just a night where you put the world to rights.

Now they had put their worlds to rights.

'I don't want to tell people yet,' Freya said. 'I am the happiest ever but I want some time to get used to the idea and—' she rolled her eyes '—don't get me started on my parents.'

'Okay, we shan't tell anyone, though you'll start to show fairly soon.'

'No.' Freya shook her head. 'I meant all of it. I meant I need to get used to the idea of us.'

'The idea?' Zack checked.

'That you love me.'

'Get used to it,' Zack said. 'But I get it.'

It was like being handed a prized package and

being told to sign for it, the start of a life he had never imagined.

'I'm such a difficult person,' Freya said. 'Don't say I didn't warn you.'

'Freya, I'm so glad I saw you raw the other night. I don't care how much you try to change, or control me, or rush me with my thoughts. You can't.' He smiled. 'You can keep on being you and I'm just going to keep on being me.'

'You're sure?'

'Completely.'

Zack took on the hardest hearts. Ones that others shied away from. But the hardest hearts gave the sweetest rewards and ones that were just so unexpected, because, for all she wanted to keep them quiet for now, on a night that should be just about them, Freya offered to share the happiness around.

'Tell your parents,' Freya said, 'when you video with them.'

'I'm not speaking to them tonight. That was just a ruse to get you here.'

'Tell them,' Freya said.

'Now?' Zack raised an eyebrow. 'I set up a romantic dinner and you want me to speak to my parents?'

Life changes.

Zack rang them and told them to get on the computer and they did.

'Here's the reason I didn't think I could come home in April,' Zack said, and he pulled Freya onto his knee.

'Hi, Freya!' they both shouted.

'They know about me?'

'I told them that there was someone special in my life,' Zack said.

That he had told them about her told Freya that this was real.

'Freya and I shall be home for Christmas, and hopefully with twins.'

'Zack!'

Oh, there was an exclamation mark at the end of his name for a reason.

Freya held up the ultrasound and watched his father put his glasses on, and it was such a precious moment.

'He's having twins,' Zack's father said to his

wife and then recovered. 'I mean you are, Freya. I just don't know what to say.'

'We thought he was gay,' Judy confessed.

'Well, I'm pleased to say he's not.' Freya laughed and realised that must have been his mother's reaction when he'd told them about her.

It was a very nice meet-the-parents and after a few moments Zack told them that, unlike in Australia, it was still Valentine's Day in LA, and he was getting back to his.

'Thanks for that,' Zack said, and as he closed the laptop she remained on his knee. 'Well, I guess we've both made it a special Valentine's Day, even if you forgot.'

'I didn't,' Freya lied. 'And I do have something for you.'

She opened up her phone and found a photo and they both smiled as they looked upon the night their world had changed.

A perfect shot.

Almost.

Save a man coming down the stairs and walking over everyone just to be by her side.

'I'm going to love you for ever,' Zack said, and it wasn't a revelation.

They knew.

'I'm going to be busy doing the same,' Freya said.

This was love.

* * * * *

MILLS & BOON®
Large Print Medical

November

Tempted by Hollywood's Top Doc	Louisa George
Perfect Rivals...	Amy Ruttan
English Rose in the Outback	Lucy Clark
A Family for Chloe	Lucy Clark
The Doctor's Baby Secret	Scarlet Wilson
Married for the Boss's Baby	Susan Carlisle

December

The Prince and the Midwife	Robin Gianna
His Pregnant Sleeping Beauty	Lynne Marshall
One Night, Twin Consequences	Annie O'Neil
Twin Surprise for the Single Doc	Susanne Hampton
The Doctor's Forbidden Fling	Karin Baine
The Army Doc's Secret Wife	Charlotte Hawkes

January

Taming Hollywood's Ultimate Playboy	Amalie Berlin
Winning Back His Doctor Bride	Tina Beckett
White Wedding for a Southern Belle	Susan Carlisle
Wedding Date with the Army Doc	Lynne Marshall
Capturing the Single Dad's Heart	Kate Hardy
Doctor, Mummy...Wife?	Dianne Drake

MILLS & BOON®
Large Print Medical

February

Seduced by the Sheikh Surgeon	Carol Marinelli
Challenging the Doctor Sheikh	Amalie Berlin
The Doctor She Always Dreamed Of	Wendy S. Marcus
The Nurse's Newborn Gift	Wendy S. Marcus
Tempting Nashville's Celebrity Doc	Amy Ruttan
Dr White's Baby Wish	Sue MacKay

March

A Daddy for Her Daughter	Tina Beckett
Reunited with His Runaway Bride	Robin Gianna
Rescued by Dr Rafe	Annie Claydon
Saved by the Single Dad	Annie Claydon
Sizzling Nights with Dr Off-Limits	Janice Lynn
Seven Nights with Her Ex	Louisa Heaton

April

Waking Up to Dr Gorgeous	Emily Forbes
Swept Away by the Seductive Stranger	Amy Andrews
One Kiss in Tokyo...	Scarlet Wilson
The Courage to Love Her Army Doc	Karin Baine
Reawakened by the Surgeon's Touch	Jennifer Taylor
Second Chance with Lord Branscombe	Joanna Neil

MILLS & BOON®

Why shop at millsandboon.co.uk?

Each year, thousands of romance readers find their perfect read at millsandboon.co.uk. That's because we're passionate about bringing you the very best romantic fiction. Here are some of the advantages of shopping at www.millsandboon.co.uk:

* **Get new books first**—you'll be able to buy your favourite books one month before they hit the shops

* **Get exclusive discounts**—you'll also be able to buy our specially created monthly collections, with up to 50% off the RRP

* **Find your favourite authors**—latest news, interviews and new releases for all your favourite authors and series on our website, plus ideas for what to try next

* **Join in**—once you've bought your favourite books, don't forget to register with us to rate, review and join in the discussions

Visit **www.millsandboon.co.uk**
for all this and more today!